KNOCKED UP... AGAIN!

AN ACCIDENTAL PREGNANCY ROMANCE

LILIAN MONROE

Copyright © 2017 All rights reserved.

No part of this book may be reproduced or transmitted in any form or by any means without written permission from the author except for short quotations used for the purpose of reviews.

Resemblance to action persons, things living or dead, locales, or events is entirely coincidental.

∽

If you'd like access to the Lilian Monroe Freebie Central, which includes bonus chapters from all my books (including this one), just follow the link below:

http://www.lilianmonroe.com/subscribefront

Lilian
xox

1
JESS

My grandmother's old house hasn't changed a bit. Well, the paint is peeling a little and it's faded over the years. There are a few more weeds in the flower beds but apart from that, it looks exactly the same.

I park the car and grab my bag. I packed light—there's no one to impress in this town. In any case, Gram will probably want to stuff me so full of food I'll need a new wardrobe by the time my ten day trip is over.

My steps are light as I make my way up the flagstone path toward the wide front porch. I remember playing on the path, skipping from flagstone to flagstone when I was a kid, over and back for hours at a time. I grin as I place my feet on the stones and avoid the bits of grass that stick up between them. Old habits die hard, I guess.

By the time I make it to the porch and put my foot on the first rickety step, the screen door swings open.

"Jessica," my grandmother's warm voice greets me. Her wrinkled face is lit up with a huge smile, and she steps out to spread her arms wide.

"Hi, Gram." I hop up the steps and drop my bag before

wrapping my grandmother in a huge bear hug. "It's good to see you."

She smiles at me and strokes my cheek with a gnarled finger. "Good to see you too, darling. Come on in. Is that all you brought?"

"Just the one bag."

She nods and her eyebrow shoots up. "Well all right. Your old room is all made up. You put your things down and come to the kitchen for some food."

She gives my arm a squeeze and flashes me another smile and then disappears down the hallway toward the kitchen. I take a few moments to glance around and smile. Nothing's changed. To the right is the living room with the old overstuffed sofa that we weren't allowed to sit on when we were kids. Straight ahead is the creaky stairway up to the bedrooms with the white handrail curling around at the bottom in a graceful arc. I run my fingers along the wainscoting at waist height and take in the old paisley wallpaper that must be older than I am.

I'm home.

My room hasn't changed at all. From the time I moved in when I was seven to the time I moved out when I was eighteen, this was my refuge. The small single bed with the floral bedspread is still in the corner, and my favorite teddy bear is carefully placed in front of the pillows. I drop my bag and pick the faded brown bear up.

"Hey, Mr. Tickles. How have you been?"

Mr. Tickles looks back at me with his glassy eyes and I bring him up to my nose. I breathe in deeply and sigh. I spent hours hugging that bear until I fell asleep when I was a little girl. I put him back down on the bed and scan the room. My medals from sports, the trophy I won in a debate tournament, the certificates of achievement for schoolwork—it's all displayed exactly how I had it when I was here. I shake my head. Gram must have thought I was going to move back in eventually.

There wasn't a hope on Earth that I'd move back in. Lexington, Virginia isn't exactly the belly button of the universe, and it certainly wasn't the most pleasant place for me to grow up. Apart from Gram who loved me unconditionally, I was always an outsider here. I got out as soon as that college acceptance letter came through.

The stairs creak as I make my way back to the kitchen. I step through the door and let it swing back and forth behind me. Gram looks over her shoulder.

"Come here, dear. I've made some chicken for you. Grab a plate."

"Smells delicious, Gram."

"Just simple cooking," she responds as she spoons the fragrant meat onto my plate. "You look as thin as a rail, Jessica. Eat up."

I laugh and shake my head. "You're always trying to fatten me up, Gram."

"You young people need food. It's good for you."

I grab a knife and fork and sit down at the kitchen table. Gram keeps working away, stirring and cleaning and hustling and bustling around the kitchen. I take my first bite and groan.

"This is so good," I say.

"Do they not have chicken in New York?"

"They have chicken," I laugh, "but not your chicken."

"Mm." That's all the response I get as Gram looks over to make sure I'm eating my fill. It would be hard not to, I haven't had anything this tasty in months.

"So what's new in town? There must be some news?"

"Oh, not much. Old Mr. Wilson died, and Mrs. Wilson looks like she's on the way out. Jack Hanson's daughter is getting married to a boy from Clivestown. Melanie Sanders just had a baby boy, the most precious little baby you've ever seen."

"Deaths, weddings and babies, huh," I reply as I take another bite.

"That's life, Jessica," Gram responds as she finally pulls out a chair to sit down. "How about you? When am I going to meet the lucky man who snagged you?"

I laugh. "No one's been that lucky, Gram. You know I'd tell you if I was seeing someone. I think I'm destined to be an old maid."

"Nonsense. You're smart and beautiful and kind. Surely there's someone in that big city that means something to you?"

"Not yet," I laugh. "Not a man, anyways. I'm not in any rush to get married Gram. And you know me, I'm not interested in having kids."

Gram makes a noise and nods her head. "You might change your mind when the right man comes along," she says with a smile.

I shake my head. "Doubt it. I'm not bringing a kid into this world, it's too miserable. I wouldn't do that to an innocent child."

This time, Gram's face crinkles up and she starts laughing. "It's always been doom and gloom with you, Jessica. You haven't changed a bit."

"I prefer to call it realism," I reply as I scrape my plate for the last bits of sauce. I glance at my grandmother and smile. She takes my plate. "I'll get that, Gram. Let me do something to help."

"Don't worry about it, dear. You go see your friends. I know Samantha is dying to see you."

"I was thinking you and I would hang out tonight, Gram. I haven't seen you in so long."

Gram smiles and plants a kiss on my cheek. "You should go out and enjoy yourself. It's Friday night! There's a new owner at the Lexington Hotel. He's having some big dinner or concert or party over there tonight. Lots of young people and such. You should go. The new owner is some big shot from New York, maybe you know him."

A party at the Lex. Great.

I snort. "Doubt it. It's a bit bigger than this town, Gram. What happened to Mrs. Carter? Why did she sell the hotel?"

"When Hank died, I think a part of her died with him and she just wanted to get rid of the place," Gram replies. "That's how it goes with us old folks. Me too, but I'm just too stubborn to die," she adds with a smile.

"You're not dying anytime soon, Gram."

"Mm-hmm. Now go. The whole town will be there, you'll see everyone."

"Get all the hellos out of the way tonight, then I can just lay low for the rest of the week."

Gram laughs. "Go, my little social butterfly." She wraps me in one of her hugs again and plants a big kiss on my cheek. "It's good to see you, Jessica."

"It's good to see you too, Gram. I missed you."

"Go and have fun. I'll see you in the morning." Her eyes crinkle as she smiles at me and I wrap my arms around her in another hug. Even if Lexington never felt like home, my grandmother's arms always did.

2

JESS

It's nice to be back in the warm weather. There's quite a bit of a nip in the air, but that's to be expected at the end of April. New York is still freezing cold this time of year so this feels almost balmy. I wrap my jacket around me a little bit tighter and walk down toward Main Street.

The streets are so quiet here. Compared to the big city where everyone is in a rush and there's constant noise of cars and honking and yelling, it's almost shocking to be somewhere like this. It feels like a different universe. I glance up at the sky and see the first stars start to twinkle as dusk falls.

I take a deep breath and let the clean air fill my lungs as I turn onto Main Street. When I exhale, I can see my breath for a second before it dissipates and I take a couple deep breaths just to watch them disappear.

The hotel comes into view just down the road—it must be absolutely packed. Every man and their dog are probably there. The new owner has put lights up on all the eaves and painted the whole thing. It looks like there's a new sign, too. I speed up slightly, curious to see what else has changed.

As I get closer, the noise gets louder. It sounds like live

music and the whole town talking and shouting and singing. There's a huge banner over the front door: *Grand Re-Opening.*

Very grand, I think with a grin. I don't think the Lex could be described as 'Grand' even if the Queen of England decided to buy it.

"Well, if it isn't Jessica Lee," comes a voice to the left and a chill goes down my spine. It's the voice that bullied me all throughout high school for being a nerd, or a tomboy, or whatever it was that made me not fit in here. Miss Popularity.

"Mary Hanson," I reply. "I heard you're getting married. Congratulations." My voice sounds flat even to my ears.

"Thank you," she says, extending her hand and wiggling her fingers at me. The huge rock on her finger glimmers in the light and I nod.

"Nice ring."

"Oh, thank you," she replies, pulling her hand back and admiring the ring on her perfectly manicured hand. "He did well."

"Mm," I say, glancing around for a way to extract myself from the conversation. "Who's the lucky guy?"

"He's a gem," she replies as she flicks her long blonde hair over her shoulder and giggles. "No pun intended."

Either that or he's gotten a lobotomy and doesn't realize what he's getting himself into.

"How about you?" She asks innocently. "Any wedding bells or are you still all *alone*?"

I bristle. "Living the single life in the big city," I reply. "Tinder's number 1 user."

Mary purses her lips and nods. "Well you haven't changed a bit."

I say nothing, trying to ignore the thinly veiled insult. I paint a smile on my face as the anger starts to swell in my chest. She flicks her hair behind her shoulder and smirks.

"How long are you in town for?" She finally asks to break the silence. She doesn't try to conceal the look of disdain as her eyes scan me from head to toe. A small part of me wishes I was wearing something nicer than jeans, a tank top and a plain jacket and I hate myself for thinking it.

"Ten days," I reply. "Visiting Gram for Easter."

"Well you *have* to come by for dinner one night. I have *so much* to tell you."

"I'm sure you do. Sounds good, I'll see you then!" I turn to the hotel entrance and slip inside before she can make any real plans with me. Dinner with Mary Hanson and the poor soul who's marrying her sounds like my idea of Hell.

The noise inside the hotel is loud. There's a band on stage and people dancing like maniacs. The bar is packed with familiar faces and the whole place is decorated in balloons, garlands, and little lights on all the rafters.

My eyes scan the room and a smile starts forming on my lips. I shake my shoulders and try to forget about Mary Hanson.

She disappears from my head completely when someone steps beside me. I smell his cologne before anything else. It smells almost spicy, but with a surprising freshness. Like a magnet pulling my head, I turn to see the most incredible looking man I've ever seen in my life. I think he stepped out of GQ Magazine and into the Lexington Hotel by accident. My body tenses immediately and I can't see anything but him.

He's staring at me with eyes the color of mahogany. His lips are plump and perfect, and there's a hint of stubble over his strong jaw. His hair is dark brown and styled effortlessly.

"Do I know you?" He asks, tilting his head slightly and then licking his lips.

His words almost don't register, because I'm too busy

staring at his lips. They move just a bit when he speaks, and then spread into a small smile. His voice is as smooth as butter and it pierces through my chest and sends a thrill straight through my stomach.

I clear my throat. "Uh, no. No, I don't think so."

"I'm Owen," he says and his voice almost makes me fall over. He raises his hand toward me and on autopilot, I slip mine into it.

"Jessica," I reply. It comes out as a croak just as our palms touch. Another thrill goes down my spine and I inhale sharply. His hand is warm and wide and it covers my palm completely. His hands feel... not rough, exactly, but solid. We stay like that for a second that lasts an eternity until he smiles again.

"Enjoy your evening, Jessica."

"Call me Jess. I will. Thanks. You too."

"Jess," he replies as if he's tasting my name in his mouth. My whole body buzzes as my name leaves his lips.

His fingers slip away and he looks at me one last time before turning and weaving his way through the crowd. He's a good six inches taller than most people, and as wide as a football player, but he slides through the crowd almost gracefully. It's like they part around him like a school of fish around a shark without even noticing what they're doing.

I'm pulled out of my daze by another voice.

"Jess! You met our sexy new mystery owner!" I smile and turn to see the familiar freckled face of my oldest and kindest friend.

"I guess I did. How are you, Sam?"

She wraps me in a hug and laughs. "It's great to see you. You look amazing!"

It's my turn to laugh. "Doubt it, but thanks. Come on, let

me buy you a drink and you can tell me everything I've missed."

She snorts. "That'll be a quick conversation. You haven't missed a thing."

I laugh as we turn to the bar, and I can't help glancing back toward the place in the crowd where Owen disappeared. My hand tingles where he touched it as I turn back to Sam and smile. She's right about one thing, he's definitely mysterious, and undeniably sexy.

3

OWEN

I NEVER THOUGHT MOVING to a small town would be easy but I didn't think it would be this hard. It's possible that New Yorkers might actually be more welcoming than this place. When I first arrived, news had travelled far that there was a new owner of the Lexington Hotel and I got the immediate sense that there were lots of people that weren't too happy about it.

Even tonight, with the whole town out to celebrate the grand re-opening, I see a lot of sideways glances.

I've heard a lot of the rumors about me. I'm some billionaire, running away from a sordid past. They say my wife left me, or she died, or I killed her. They say I don't have a wife, and that the loneliness drove me to leave New York. They say I stole my money and now I need someplace to bury it so the IRS doesn't come after me.

They say I coerced Gladys Carter into selling the hotel, but the truth is she approached my real estate agent. She was desperate to sell, and I saw an opportunity.

That's what I do.

I take opportunities and I make them work. That's how I

made my money. That's why I left New York. That's why I'll leave this place as soon as I see another opportunity.

I'm not some dark, mysterious billionaire out to swindle kind townsfolk. I'm just a guy with a pocketful of cash and a particular skill at turning that into more cash. That's my story whenever anyone asks, anyways.

Sure, I've got skeletons in my closet, but who doesn't? Whatever was going on in New York is behind me now.

That blonde woman walks back into the hotel and our eyes meet for a brief second—what's her name again? Mary something? She raises her hands and wiggles her fingers at me while batting her eyelashes. I dip my chin down slightly. For a woman that's about to get married, she sure does throw a lot of glances around the room.

I turn away from her and pray that she doesn't come toward me. I lean against one of the old timber pillars that line the outside of the room and run my fingers through my hair. The townspeople love to gossip, but they certainly didn't refuse an invitation. There are people everywhere dancing, talking, drinking, shouting. You might even call tonight a success. My eyes scan the bar for the other woman, the one I've never seen before.

Jess.

That's one name I won't forget. There she is. She's at the bar with another girl, the friendly freckle-faced girl that helped me when I got a flat tire last week. They're laughing. Jess throws her head back and her whole body doubles over as she laughs at something the other girl said. She wipes a tear from her eye and I lean forward, as if I'd be able to hear what they're saying from over here.

Then, she lifts her eyes as if they were drawn to me. I can see that spark in them that I saw earlier. There's a hint of a smile on her lips and all of a sudden, it's just me and her. I can't hear the band. I can't see a single other person, or hear the shouting of two hundred voices. It's just me and her, eyes locked on each other from opposite ends of the room.

It feels like we're on a moving train, and everything and everyone in the room is whipping past at a hundred miles an hour except for her. I can almost smell that floral perfume she was wearing.

Then, she turns her head to her friend and I'm rocked back into the real world. My heart's racing and I blink three or four times. I realize I'm holding a bottle of beer and I bring the cold liquid to my lips.

What just happened?

I need to find out who she is.

I can't help myself. My eyes swing back to her. One of the young guys from town is walking up to her and she greets him warmly. She opens her arms and they hug for what seems like an eternity. Jealousy starts curdling in my stomach as I watch them pull apart, and then she runs her hands over his arms. Everyone laughs and I wish I knew what it was about.

They stop touching each other and my shoulders immediately relax. I turn away from them and take another angry sip of beer.

What the fuck is wrong with me?

I don't know this woman! I just learned her name three minutes ago. And now I'm jealous that she gave some guy a hug? She seems to know everyone and has more people coming to say hello. She's obviously been away and has just come back—of course she'd hug everyone. They're probably her childhood friends, for Christ's sake.

Fuck me.

I'm being ridiculous. I turn around and walk toward the

back. I need to get out of this room, to get away from her and stop fucking staring at her.

I stalk to the back of the room, weaving between people and finally making it to the narrow door that says "Staff Only". I push it open and step through, closing it behind me with a slam. I slump onto my office chair and put my head in my hands.

This isn't me.

Women don't have that effect on me. Jealous? Of some redneck country boy? Over some woman I literally don't even know?

This isn't why I came here. I came here to get away from New York, to get away from my family's business and try to start something for myself. I didn't come here to get involved with anyone in this tiny town.

I need to get a grip. I take a couple deep breaths and blow all the air out of my lungs. There's a stack of invoices next to my computer that need to be sorted, so I pick up the first one and fire up my laptop. Nothing like some boring old numbers to cool me down after... whatever it was that just happened to me out there.

4

JESS

"Do you remember the day that I caught that frog and you were so worried about it that you stole it and set it free behind my back?" Sam's brother, Cory, laughs. "You were so worried about that little thing!"

"It was an innocent animal!" I protest, laughing. "You were going to hold it hostage for who knows how long! And probably torture it, you psychopath."

"And the truth didn't come out until about five years later," Sam adds. She shakes her head and grins at me. "You always had a bleeding heart, Jess."

"That's me," I respond with a laugh. "Empathy is my middle name. Or it was, until I moved to New York and became an asshole."

"Stop it, Jess," Cory says with a grin. "You're just the same as you were when you arrived in Lexington. Just a scared little girl at heart."

I smack his arm and laugh. "Shut up Cory. Don't you have some girls to go annoy or are you going to hang around with your sister and her friends the whole night?"

"You're right, I'm wasting time. Better make the rounds.

You comin' around for dinner tomorrow night? Mom's making a roast beef."

"Wouldn't miss it for the world," I respond. He leans in to kiss my cheek and then turns toward the room.

"Your brother hasn't changed a bit," I say as I turn to Sam. I take a sip of the cheap beer in my hand as Sam laughs.

"Not one bit. He never will," she replies, shaking her head and watching as he sits down at a table full of women uninvited. "Don't know how we came out of the same woman, to be honest."

She turns to me and gives me a grin. My eyebrows shoot up.

"What!"

She raises an eyebrow and takes a sip of the brown bottle of beer in her hand. "Seems like you've got an admirer."

I laugh and shake my head, confused. "What are you talking about?"

"I saw you two looking at each other from across the room."

"Who!" I exclaim, knowing exactly who she's talking about.

"You know exactly who I'm talking about, Jessica Lee." She says it just like Gram used to say when I was in trouble, with the same head shake and finger wag. I laugh.

"What! We just happened to make eye contact. Pff. Admirer," I say, staring down at my bottle.

"Happened to make eye contact?" She exclaims. "Please. Happened to make eye contact and then happened to keep staring at each other for all of eternity. I was practically ready to leave by the time you finished."

"Stop it," I say, still laughing. "Who is he anyways? He told me his name was Owen."

"Oh so you're on a first name basis now, are you? Moving a bit quickly, don't you think?"

"Shut up, Sam," I say with a laugh. She grins and I see those little dimples on either side of her cheeks that I used to be so jealous of. "What's his story, anyways?"

"No one really knows," she says, glancing around the room. I follow her gaze and realize he must have disappeared somewhere when I wasn't looking. I frown as Sam continues. "He bought the place up without even seeing it, and then showed up and started renovating it. No one even knew it was up for sale before construction started. Caused quite the stir."

"I can imagine. People don't like change around here."

"They sure don't, unless that change is a wedding or a baby."

"So he's from New York?"

"That's what they say. I've heard all sorts of stories about him, but I wouldn't pay attention to them. Mary Hanson told me he'd killed his wife and was running from the police."

I snort. "She did not."

"She did. I had that same reaction and asked her if she thought buying the only hotel for fifty miles was a good way of laying low. She just walked away and hasn't said a word to me in two weeks."

I laugh. "You're better off."

"I'm not complaining," Sam responds with a grin. She checks her watch and sighs. "I'd better go. Ma's not doing great at home on her own, so I'll have to help her into bed. You're coming for dinner for sure tomorrow? Bring your grandmother over as well."

"I will," I respond and give Sam a warm hug. "It's good to see you, Sam."

"Good to see you too. Behave yourself now, you hear me?"

"I'll try," I respond with a laugh. She winks at me and

slips away through the crowd. I lean back against the bar and take another sip of my drink, trying to figure out if I'm happy to be back or not. It's nice to see familiar faces, but I can feel the onslaught of memories starting to creep in. Suddenly the room seems stuffy, or overly crowded. I finish my beer and head to the washrooms. Maybe I just need to splash some water on my face.

5

OWEN

I TYPE the last invoice into my spreadsheet and file the paper away. With a sigh, I hit 'save' and lean back in my chair. It's probably time to go make some rounds again and try to interact with these people. They already think I'm an outsider, isolating myself with work while everyone is drinking and having fun will only make it worse.

My chair drags on the floor as I push it back and I close the laptop screen as I get up. The muffled noise of the band gets suddenly louder as I pull the office door open. Just as I'm about to step out into the main room, a body crashes into mine and I stumble backward.

"Oh! Sorry! I thought this was the bathroom! Are you okay?"

"I'm fine. It's okay! Are you okay?"

It's her. It takes me a few seconds to regain my composure. I take a step back and stare at her flushed face. She glances at me and then away.

"Yeah, I'm good. Sorry. I thought this was the bathroom," she says again. "I haven't been here in a few years."

We fall silent for a few moments and she swings her eyes back to me. We just stare at each other for a few breaths.

"So are you from here?" I ask slowly. She hasn't made a move to leave and every atom in my body is screaming for her to stay. I take a step back and pick up a bottle of whiskey off the shelf. I lift it up toward her and raise an eyebrow.

The hint of a grin spreads on her face. She nods her chin down a fraction of an inch and takes a step inside before closing the door behind her.

"Yeah, I grew up here from the time I was seven. Left for New York a few years ago and I come back once in a while to see my grandma."

I nod. "I lived in New York for years." I pull out two tumbler glasses and pour a bit of whiskey in them. "I don't have ice over here, sorry."

She shrugs and takes one of the glasses, clinking it against mine. I lean back against the desk and bring the glass up to my lips. She takes a sip and grimaces. "I'll never get used to that taste."

She sits down across from me and crosses her legs. Her jeans are skin-tight, hugging every curve of her body perfectly. She tilts her head to the side.

"So I hear you're a wife murderer, here to run away from the police. Or is it the IRS you're running from? I can't remember."

I laugh. "One or the other. I never knew I'd done such horrible things until people started telling me about them."

She chuckles and takes another sip. "It's one of the reasons I left. The rumor mill in this place is insatiable. They can be very cruel."

Her face darkens for a moment and then she shakes her head. I want to ask her what happened but the words catch in my throat. Before I can say anything, she waves a hand around and grins.

"I like what you've done with the place."

"It's amazing what a few lights and some paint will do," I respond. "You wouldn't believe the amount of grief I've gotten over it though. You'd have thought I tore down the whole thing and put in a high rise."

She laughs and shakes her head. "That's one thing around here you'll have to get used to. People are more afraid of change than they are of dying."

"That's probably true of most places," I respond. I take another sip and watch her over the rim of my glass. Her tank top is clinging to her body and all I want to do is run my fingers over her stomach. Her collarbone is calling out to me, begging to be tasted. I take a deep breath and move my eyes to meet hers.

"Why do you look at me like that?" She asks. The question surprises me.

"Like what?"

"Like you just did. You look at me like… I don't know. Like you're noticing every detail. You're intense."

"Intense," I repeat. "I haven't gotten that one before."

"You're avoiding the question."

How could I not avoid the question? What would I say? That I'm looking at her like I want to wrap my arms around her and taste those perfect lips of hers? Maybe I could tell her that her body is making my cock throb or that I haven't been this aware of my heartbeat in years.

"I'm observant," I finally reply.

She laughs, and once again I'm surprised. "I get why people around here think all kinds of things about you."

"What's that supposed to mean?"

I don't know whether to be offended or turned on right

now. I've never met anyone like her. I never know what she's going to say or how she's going to say it. I'm hanging on every word and I simultaneously love and despise the feeling.

"It means you don't say what you mean. Everything you say sounds like a riddle."

"It isn't. I haven't said anything that wasn't true."

"But you haven't said anything that is true either," she shoots back. I stare at her for a second and her sharp hazel eyes sparkle for a moment. She drains the rest of her glass and stands up. "Thanks for the drink."

She places the tumbler next to me on the desk and I catch a whiff of her perfume again. I nod and watch her as she turns around and walks out the office. The door shuts with a soft click and I'm alone again.

For the second time tonight I blow all the air out of my lungs. I need to see her again.

6
JESS

The washroom is the next door down, and I duck in quickly. The relative quiet of the toilets seems strange after the noise of the bar. I head to the sink and splash some water on my face.

My heart is racing and I feel flushed. I don't remember someone ever having that effect on me. I pat my face dry and take a deep breath.

He's so incredibly sexy. I could hardly breathe when he was that close to me. The way he was looking at me was making my whole center throb. I had to get out before I did something I'd regret.

I jump as the washroom door swings open. Mary Hanson steps through with a smirk on her face and I stifle a groan.

"Hi, Mary."

"Well aren't you getting familiar with the new stranger in town."

"What?" I guess it doesn't take long for rumors to start around here. Mary just laughs.

"Don't pretend. I saw you going into the office together. You don't waste any time, do you. You haven't changed a bit."

"Oh fuck right off, Mary!"

The anger explodes inside me and I brush past her, punching the door open and storming out. The tears are prickling against my eyelids and my vision has gone blurry as I stumble across the dance floor toward the exit. Her words replay in my head as I bump into one person after another trying to get to the exit.

Finally, the fresh air fills my lungs and I jog down the three porch steps to the street. I stomp down Main Street toward Gram's house without looking back.

How many people saw me go into his office? How many people saw me come out of the bathroom practically crying?

Mary's snarling face is burned into my mind and I shake my head to try and dispel it. My feet carry me back to Gram's house and I tiptoe up the stairs before collapsing in bed.

I should have left with Sam. Now the talk of the town won't be Owen buying up the Lex, it'll be me sneaking off into the office with him at the grand opening. Mary's probably told half the town by now.

Tears start welling up in my eyes again as I remember the months before I left for the first time. I remember the torture of walking around knowing there were eyes on my back wherever I went. I remember hearing a new rumor about me every day, and how everything I did was twisted and distorted until I felt like I was driving myself crazy.

I thought I was passed that. I thought I'd moved on, moved to the big city, and left Mary Hanson and her wagging tongue behind me, but here I am. I'm walking down the same streets with the same tears rolling down my cheeks about something that someone said to so-and-so and then someone else said this.

Why do I care! So I had a conversation with a man who was new in town! So he happens to be incredibly attractive and every time his eyes met mine it sent a thrill down my spine. So what! Let Mary Hanson say whatever she likes, I'll talk to whoever I want.

I brush the tears away from my eyes when I hear footsteps creaking on the old wooden floorboards toward my room. Gram's voice calls out softly through the door.

"You okay, dear? How was the Lex?"

I sit up in bed and wipe my eyes again. "It was fine, Gram." I get up and open the door. She's wearing her housecoat and looks exhausted. "I didn't mean to wake you."

"You didn't wake me, honey. I couldn't sleep."

A grin spreads on my face. "Grammy, were you waiting up for me to get home?"

"No, no. Of course not. It's just these old bones not wanting to sleep tonight." She glances up at me and I see her lips curl upward.

"Gram, you know that I'm almost twenty-nine years old, right? And I've lived on my own for over a decade? I think I'll be okay in this town for a night." I laugh. "You should have slept."

She waves her hand and shakes her head from side to side. "Shh. Old habits, Jessica. I'm glad you're back safe. Give me a kiss."

I kiss her cheeks and she wraps her frail arms around me. "See you in the morning."

"See you in the morning, Gram. Have a sleep-in tomorrow, okay?"

"Mm," she responds. I watch her go back to her room and close the door. She seems to move a bit slower these days, and her wrinkles are a bit deeper. She's still the same, just a bit older. I know she'll be up with the sun like she is every day. I shake my head and close my bedroom door.

At least tomorrow will be dinner with Sam's family. If I'm

lucky I won't run into Mary Hanson or anyone else who lives on half-truths and rumors.

7

OWEN

I wake up with the sun streaming through the window directly into my eyes. I groan and turn around before dragging myself up out of bed. I really need to buy blinds for this room. I glance out the window onto Main Street and see the empty beer bottles and cigarette butts all along the hotel porch below me. We didn't have time to clean everything before passing out last night.

I sigh. Living in the hotel is great, except for the fact that I'm always at work. I walk to the bathroom and turn on the shower until it's scalding and then step in. I smell like stale beer and cigarette smoke, and I want to scrub myself clean.

As the water hits my body, I think of Jess as she sat in the chair in my office. I wonder what she's doing right now and how long she'll be in town. She could be gone for all I know. I scrub my body and start washing my hair and my thoughts drift back to her long legs and the way her eyes glimmered when she spoke. My cock throbs and I try to ignore it.

That spark inside her makes me want to know more. I want to see her again and talk to her again. I want to ask her what happened to her before she left here, and why she left, and why she's back. I want to ask her about New York and her life there.

I have so many questions and I still know nothing about her.

Once I'm clean, I turn the shower off and grab a towel. I sigh, wiping the condensation off the mirror to drag a comb through my hair.

Jess pops into my mind again and I wonder if I'll see her today. I sigh, shaking my head to stop thinking about her. I have things to do, I can't keep obsessing over some chick that's visiting her grandmother. I finish in the bathroom and throw some clothes on before heading down the creaky old steps to the main floor. The lobby is newly renovated with fresh paint and a new carpet, and to the left is the bar. I push the door open and sigh. The place is a disaster.

"Morning, Joe," I call out to the bartender. He's restocking his shelves and I start gathering empty bottles off the tables. "Got pretty crazy in here last night."

"Mm-hmm," is the only response I get. I move from table to table until everything is picked up and then move on to the floor.

It feels good to get my hands dirty. This project has been different to all my other investments. Usually I'm just managing the money, and I oversee the renovations or work and then sell for a profit, but not this place. Mrs. Carter warned me about it when I bought the hotel off her. She said I'd need to be involved or else the townspeople wouldn't trust me. I'm only just starting to realize how true that is.

I don't mind though. It stops me thinking about New York. When I left, my father's business was under investigation and I'd just narrowly avoided prosecution. The trial of the decade, they've been calling it. At least in Lexington my name and face aren't plastered over every newspaper and TV channel, and I don't have cameras stuck in my face all the time.

Here, my notoriety has nothing to do with my father or his finances. I get talked about because I decided to change the color of the carpet in the lobby, or because I put up new lights outside the hotel. I can deal with that kind of notoriety. No one knows my father, and no one cares about big city politics.

I grab a broom and start sweeping up the floor. Joe gets the mop and follows behind me until the whole place is clean again. Joe leans against the mop and turns to me.

"You did good last night," he says. "Folks will be happy about the way you opened this place back up."

"Thanks Joe. I tried to keep the original charm of the hotel, and I hope they could see that."

"Mm-hmm," he says again, lifting the mop back into the bucket. "Whatever they say about you, you're all right."

I chuckle. "Thanks."

He just nods and wheels the mop away. Somehow that small compliment seems like it means a lot more. It's like a seal of approval. I brush my hands together and sweep my eyes around the room, sighing in satisfaction.

I might be able to make this place work after all. I don't need my father's money, or my father's business to back me. I can do this on my own!

I grab a big garbage bag and head to the front door to clean up the porch. I swing them open, putting a door stopper in front of one of them.

"Morning, Mr. McAllister!"

I turn my head to see Mary Hanson heading out of the corner store across the road.

"Morning, Mary. Hope you enjoyed yourself last night."

"Oh it was a great night. And I see you enjoyed yourself as

well," she replies, crossing the road and standing with her hand on her hip. Somehow it seems like there's a double meaning to her words. I frown.

"I did, yeah. It was great to see everyone come out and support the re-opening."

"That's not what I meant," she says slowly. "But it *was* great to see everyone."

"And what did you mean?"

She laughs as the skin around her eyes tightens. "I meant when you disappeared into your office with Jessica Lee. You be careful with her. Have a good day now!"

She wiggles her fingers in goodbye and I frown as she turns back to her car. My heart starts thumping in my chest and I turn slowly to look at the mess on the porch. One by one, I drop the empty bottles and ashtray contents into the garbage bags as I turn her words over in my head.

Be careful with Jess? Does she think we slept together? I mean, obviously she does, or at least she wants me to think she does. I hadn't even realized that anyone had seen us in there together, but at this rate it'll be the talk of the town by midday. I shake my head and take a deep breath.

Living in this town is like walking through a minefield. It's enough to drive a man insane. No wonder Jess left. Mary's words ring in my ears and all I can do is think about asking Jess what she meant. Instead of warning me off her, she's only made me want her more.

8

JESS

"Are you sure you're okay to walk over, Gram?"

"Of course, honey. I need to get these old legs moving."

"All right. Here—hold my arm."

My grandmother and I walk down the porch steps slowly. She leans against me, hooking her arm through mine as we set off toward Sam's house. Gram points out some flowers that are in bloom and I ask her the name of plants.

"The tulips are just starting to come up now, they should be out any day," she says, looking over at another perfectly manicured lawn.

"Mm," I respond, looking at the street that's all too familiar. I feel like I know every crack in the pavement, every shingle on every roof. I've walked or ran or biked between my grandmother's house and Sam's thousands of times over the years. This time, we walk at a leisurely pace, with Gram leaning against me when she needs it.

The air is clear and warm as we make our way to Main Street. Sam lives just on the edge of town, a few blocks down from the square where the Lex and the grocer are. Gram pats my arm as we turn the corner and swing the gate up to Sam's house.

Once again, the screen door opens before we get a chance to knock.

"Grandma Lee!" Sam says as she comes out to greet us. "You're looking radiant tonight. Come on in." Sam smiles and takes Gram's other arm to help her in the house. I can't help but notice how much more wheezing and panting that Gram is doing compared to last time I saw her. Her movements seem so much more labored than before, when she was just one big ball of energy. She used to be able to chase me around the house and still have energy to do everything else.

Mrs. Cooke comes out of the kitchen and opens her arms. "Jessie!" She says as she wraps me in a hug. "My second daughter!"

"Hi, Mrs. Cooke. It's good to see you."

The smile on my lips spreads to my heart as she wraps me in another hug. Between her and Gram, I had a childhood full of love once I moved here. I might have lost my own parents, but I found a second family. The two of them coaxed me out of my shell and showed me that even without a mother around, I was still loved.

Mr. Cooke appears and the greetings continue. My cheeks hurt already from smiling and we haven't even made it through the door yet. There's laughter and talking and remembering as everyone goes inside and sits down in the living room. Mrs. Cooke's food smells amazing, and I look around the old house and smile.

There's something about this town. Even for all its faults and all the gossip, even though I had to leave and get away from it all, even though I've lived in New York for almost ten years, there's still something about it. A glass of wine appears in my hand and there's more laughter, and talking, and eating.

Before I know it, the stars are twinkling in the black sky and Gram and I are saying our goodbyes. My heart feels light as I give Sam another hug.

"You want to meet for lunch tomorrow?" She asks. "There's something I want to tell you."

"What is it?" I laugh. "You're not going to leave me hanging all night, are you?"

Sam grins. "I'm going to have to. Meet around noon? Come here and I'll tell you the big news."

"The big news, eh," I say with a raised eyebrow. "So big it needs its own special lunch to announce it?"

Sam laughs. "It does, yeah. Just come over at noon, Jess, stop giving me a hard time."

"Fine," I reply with a laugh. "I'll see you tomorrow."

She shoots me that dazzling smile and I say one last thank you before turning to my grandmother. Her eyes are drooping and the lines in her face seem a mile deep. She's bone-tired.

"Gram, do you want to wait here and I'll go get the car? We can drive back together then."

"No, no, no. Don't be ridiculous. I'm fine to walk, I'm not that old. These legs have some life in them yet."

"Okay," I say, and cringe as she stumbles on the pavement. I grab her arm and help her gain her balance again. "Are you sure? I won't be long. I'll be over and back in no time and drive you back."

"Let's go, honey, I'm fine."

We start the walk back to the house. What would take me a quick ten minutes looks like it'll be a long half hour walk for the two of us. Gram is quiet now, just focused on putting one foot in front of the other. I look over at her and hold her arm a little bit tighter.

We walk in silence for a few blocks, until we get to the turn toward her house. It's taken us ten minutes or more to get this far, and Gram looks exhausted. I should have insisted we drive, but there's no arguing with her when she has her mind set on something.

We turn the corner and before I know it, her foot catches on the sidewalk and she stumbles. I cry out and immediately know I won't be able to catch her this time. She's falling away from me, and I can't get my arm around her body.

"Gram!" I yell. She stumbles again and I watch in horror as she falls toward the hard pavement.

Before she hits the ground, an arm appears and catches her. She's lifted clean off the ground and placed gently back on her feet before I know what's happening.

"You okay, Mrs. Lee?"

It's him. It's Owen. He looks from me to my grandmother with concern written all over his face. His tee-shirt is clinging to his chest and his muscles are outlined perfectly. He drags his fingers through his hair and takes a big sigh.

"My car is just around the corner. Let me drive you home." His eyes flick to me and he seems to plead with me. I nod.

"Come on, Gram."

"Yes, thank you, Mr. McAllister. That sounds lovely," she wheezes. She pats her fingers against her cheeks and then her hair and I put my arm around her shoulders.

He laughs. "For the thousandth time, call me Owen."

Gram just nods and I smile.

Thank you, I mouth to Owen. He nods once, quickly, and then jogs around the corner. Within a couple seconds I hear an engine roar to life and a pickup truck comes around the corner.

"It's just a two-door, so we'll have to squeeze in here."

"I can walk," I say just as I imagine being squeezed up against Owen's muscular body. My heart starts beating a little bit faster.

Gram snorts. "For someone who insisted on driving you sure do sound like you want to walk."

She shoots me a grin and I laugh and shake my head.

"All right."

Owen helps my grandmother into the passenger's seat and closes the door. He walks around to the driver's side toward me. I can't stop looking at his chest, and the way his tee-shirt is stretched over his arms. I had no idea he was this fit.

"Thanks, Owen. I can't tell you how much I appreciate it," I say in a low voice. Gram's head is resting against the window and she has her eyes closed already. "I tried to get her to drive but she was having none of it."

He smiles and my heart flips. "It's nothing," he replies. He sweeps his hand toward the pickup. "Your carriage awaits."

"Does that make you my knight in shining armor?"

This time his smile cracks into a laugh. "Something like that."

9

OWEN

THE FABRIC of my tee-shirt feels like sandpaper against my skin, and I can feel every tiny textured bump in the leather of my steering wheel. Jess's arm and leg are pressed up against my side and the heat of her body feels like it's burning me. Every inch of my skin is hyper sensitive right now.

Jess shifts her weight and we move a fraction of an inch further apart. My heart drops and I shake my head at how disappointed I feel.

I need to get a grip.

She lifts her hand and I watch as she gently pat's her grandmother's knee. Am I jealous of that knee right now? First, I was jealous of some other guy giving her a hug and know I'm jealous of her *grandmother*?

I sigh and try to keep my eye on the road. I'm glad this is a quiet town, because I'm having trouble focusing right now.

Jess moves again, and this time she shifts closer to me. My heart does a flip and starts bouncing against my ribcage. Her leg and arm are pressed against mine. I desperately want to lift my arm up and wrap it around her shoulder. I want to feel her head on my chest and bury my head in her hair.

"What's that?" She points at the camera on my dashboard.

"Dash-cam," I reply. "Records everything while I'm driving. I had one in New York and it saved me when I was dealing with insurance, so I swore I'd never be without one."

"This isn't exactly New York," she replies with a grin. "Very high-tech carriage you've got, Mr. Knight-in-Shining-Armor."

"Only the best for my damsels in distress."

Jess laughs and the sound makes my heart flip in my chest again. All too soon, we make the last turn and I pull up outside Mrs. Lee's house. I put the truck in park and open the door to run over to the passenger side. As soon as I slip away from Jess, I can feel every inch of skin where her body was touching. It's like she's burned me, or there's a permanent imprint on my body wherever she touched. I take a deep breath and open the passenger's side door.

Mrs. Lee takes my hand and I help her down from the seat. She sways back and forth and tries to take a step but falters.

Jess yelps and for the second time tonight, I catch the old woman just as she's about to fall. This time, she regains her footing and stands up a bit straighter.

"Thank you very much, Mr. McAllister," she says, patting my arm and turning to her front door.

"It's Owen, please," I reply. The two of us walk up the flagstone path and up the stairs as Jess goes in front of us to open the door. She holds it open and we step through. I help Mrs. Lee to the staircase where she grabs onto the bannister and then turns to me.

"You drive safe now, thank you very much. You're very kind."

"Gram, do you need any help getting—"

"I'm all right from here, honey."

And with that, she turns to the staircase and starts slowly climbing up. Jess and I stand there until she's at the top and shuffles out of view down the hallway. Jess takes a deep breath and lets out a big sigh. Her shoulders slump. She turns toward me.

"Owen, I—"

I hold up my hand. "It's nothing, really."

"It's not nothing," she continues. Her eyes are glued on mine and I can see the pain in them. Her face is drawn with worry as she glances back up the stairs where her grandmother disappeared. She takes a step toward me. Her hand brushes my arm and she lets it rest just above my elbow. My pulse quickens again and a lump forms in my throat.

"Thank you," she almost whispers.

"It's nothing," I repeat, shaking my head. We stay still for a few moments and Jess searches my face before dropping her hand.

"Do you want to come in? For a coffee or a tea?"

She looks exhausted and I desperately want to say yes, but I know I should just let her go to bed. I take a breath.

"I should let you go," I say in a low voice. Jess shakes her head.

"Really, come in." The lines on her face relax and the hint of a smile appears. "Let me repay you that drink from last night."

The corners of my mouth start drifting upward and I nod. "All right, if you put it that way…"

She chuckles and nods her head down the hallway. "Kitchen's this way." We start walking and Jess keeps talking. "I'm afraid I don't have anything stronger, so tea will have to do."

"Tea is perfect," I reply. I'd drink anything just to stay near her right now.

10

JESS

THE KETTLE BOILS and I pour the hot water into two waiting mugs. I pull out a packet of cookies and put them on the table between us.

"Thanks," Owen says with a smile. He reaches for a cookie and dips it in his tea before taking a bite. I sit down at the table and try not to stare at his lips as they surround the cookie, or the way his hands move, or how wide his shoulders are. I turn to my tea and blow the steam away.

"So how do you know my grandmother?" I ask. "You seemed pretty familiar with each other."

"I met her one day when I was working on the garden bed in front of the hotel," he replies, reaching for another cookie. I follow the cookie's path from his strong hands up to his lips before catching myself and taking a sip of tea. "I was planting some flowers and she gave me some advice. Apparently, they would have died within weeks because there was too much sun for them." He shakes his head and smiles, flicking his eyes up to me. "I didn't even know that was a thing—too much sun for flowers. I thought plants loved sun."

I laugh. "No green thumb on you?"

"Not quite," he replies. "I think I've killed every house plant I've ever owned." His pale brown eyes are glimmering in the kitchen's low light and he chuckles. "So yeah, that day she brought me to the nursery and helped me pick some better plants. She's basically redesigned the entire garden for the Lex."

I shake my head. "She never told me that!"

He shrugs. "I kept thanking her and she kept just waving me away. It seemed like it was just so normal to her to help someone out like that."

"That's how she is," I chuckle. "I've never met anyone so giving."

"You're lucky to have her," he replies.

I shake my head. "You have no idea." We're silent for a few moments and I think of the day that I met Gram for the first time when I was seven years old. All I'd known was my mother's addiction and the string of different men she brought through the house. Finally, I was taken away. Gram took me in and healed me of all the hurt and raised me as her own child. My eyes start to mist when Owen shifts in his seat. I blink and smile at him.

"Well, thank you for saving us today," I say with a smile.

He stands up and bows with a flourish. "At your service, madam."

I burst out laughing, and then cover my mouth and try to keep quiet. "I've never been called madam before."

"Miss? Ms.? Lady?"

I stand up and curtsey with a laugh. His face cracks open in a smile and we stand in front of each other.

"It doesn't really matter what you call me," I say. "It all sounds good when you say it."

His eyes flick back up to mine and my heart starts beating harder. The air between us is thick and I can't move or breathe or speak for fear of breaking the spell that's on us. His tongue slides out of his mouth to lick his lips and I feel my center heating up. I watch it trace the line of his lips and feel the heat between my legs grow hotter.

He takes a step forward and slowly moves his hand to my waist. We're like two magnets drawn toward each other. When his hand touches my side, it feels warm and strong, and I move my fingers to run gently over his hand. I run my fingers up his arm, over every rippling muscle all the way to his shoulder.

Owen moves his other hand to my cheek and tangles it into my hair. In a flash, the tension between us explodes and he's kissing me. Our lips crush together and he pulls the nape of my neck toward him. My hands fist into his hair and his other hand covers the side of my neck.

His lips crush against mine and his tongue tastes me. He groans and pulls me closer. I press my body against his and wrap my arms around his neck. He drops his hand to wrap it around my waist and pulls me into his body.

I press myself against him. He feels so broad and strong and I pull his head closer to me. He tastes incredible, like mint and pine and musk and man all rolled into one. The stubble on his face tickles my chin and I giggle, pulling away.

I bring my fingers up to his face and run them over the hint of beard.

"Prickly," I say with a smile.

"Sorry," he replies. His eyes are diving deep into mine and he pulls me in a tiny bit closer. His hand feels so wide on the small of my back as I melt into him.

"You're not sorry at all," I say, still tracing his jawline with my finger.

"Not one bit," he says with a grin. His chin dips down and he kisses me again. This time his lips meet mine slowly, gently, and his hands run down my spine to rest in the small of my back. I melt into his arms and moan. My fingers are wrapped in his hair and my whole body is pulsing.

Suddenly I realize where I am. I'm in my grandmother's kitchen with the Lexington Hotel's new owner. I pull away and put a hand to my forehead.

"Wow," I say, flicking my eyes up to him and then back down. "I..."

He stays still and stares at me as if he's studying my face. "I'm sorry, Jess, I didn't mean to..."

"No! No, it's okay. It's just... I just got carried away."

I look at him again and he nods, and then straightens himself back up. "I should get going," he says in a low voice. It reverberates through my whole body and my center pulses. "Thanks for the tea and cookies."

"Of course."

We stand there motionless for what seems like an eternity and I think—I hope, maybe—that he'll kiss me again. He lifts his arm and runs his fingers through his hair and then nods once.

"I'll see you around."

"Yeah. Thanks. You know, for everything."

"My pleasure," he responds. The words send another thrill through me and he smiles softly before nodding and walking past me to the front door. It's not until I hear it click closed and I hear his truck start up that I sink down into the chair and put my head in my hands.

Whoa.

I can still taste his lips on mine, and every part of my body that he touched feels like it's on fire. I close my eyes and imagine the way he smells, and how my body just fell into his. Why did I stop? All I wanted to do was keep kissing and kissing and kissing him and feel his hands on every part of my body.

My heartbeat finally goes back down and I pick up my mug of tea, letting the lukewarm liquid fill my mouth. I stand up to clean the dishes and realize that my panties are completely soaked through.

I sigh and close my eyes again, trying to anchor the memory of his taste, his smell, his touch.

At this rate, Mary Hanson's rumors will end up being true after all.

11

OWEN

I CAN STILL TASTE her on my lips when I drive away from the house. My heart is pounding and I squint to focus on the road. For the second time tonight, I'm grateful this town is quiet. I pull up behind the hotel and kill the engine before leaning back in my seat and closing my eyes.

Jess's body paints itself on my eyelids. I see that little smile of hers right after she finished curtseying, and the flash in her eyes when my hand touched her waist. I let out a sigh and rub my face with my hands.

I don't know what it is about this girl, but she makes my body feel like a coiled spring. Sitting in her grandmother's kitchen felt like the most intimate place to be, and we didn't even touch until she was wrapping her arms around me and pressing her curves against me.

A sharp tap on the window makes me jump and I open my eyes to see Joe standing outside my door. He frowns at me and I open the door to step out.

"You okay, boss?"

"Yeah, Joe, I'm fine," I respond. *Great, actually.* "Just tired tonight."

"Closed up early, I'm heading home." It isn't a question, and I wonder who the boss is between us. I nod.

"Sounds good. See you tomorrow."

"You take care of yourself," he says before walking off in the darkness. I watch him walk away and take another deep breath as I slam my truck door closed and spin my keyring around my finger. He's worked at the hotel for longer than I've been alive, and I've never met anyone more reliable. Joe's approval probably means more than any renovations or improvements I could ever make.

I make my way upstairs to the small room in the back corner that I've taken as my own. I flop down onto the bed and stare at the ceiling. I wonder if Jess is thinking about me right now? Did that kiss have this effect on her?

I close my eyes and imagine her again. I wonder what it would feel like to have her here beside me, to feel her body close to mine as we lay together. Even the feeling of her body under her clothes was incredible, I can't imagine what it would feel like to have her skin pressed up against mine.

This is unfamiliar. Women have always come and gone with me. Sometimes, one of them catches my eye but it always fizzles out. Sometimes it ends in an explosion and you need to run away to a small town to get away from it all, but it always ends.

Somehow, I don't want this to happen with Jess. I want to know what's behind those eyes. I want her to surprise me and make me laugh and be sarcastic and witty. I want her mind and her body. I want it all.

I want it all, and it terrifies me.

For all the gossip about me, the town rumor mill has it all wrong. I've never been married—I've never even had a long term girlfriend. I've always been too busy with business and career to think about love.

Love. Whatever that is.

It's not worth it. I learned that as a child when I saw my parent's marriage operate like a business transaction. They needed each other for money and status and that's all it was. Maybe it's better that way. Relationships are a distraction, and they lead to nothing but pain and misery.

I sit up in bed and rub my face again. I've known this girl for two days and I'm already talking myself out of a relationship with her!

I should just relax. It'll be like every other woman I've ever met. I know it will. We'll sleep together, it'll be great, and that itch will be scratched. She'll lose her charm and I'll get bored. She might get hurt or she might understand, but that's where it'll end. That's where it always ends.

It's better that way.

Once this hotel is up and running again it'll be time for me to move on to something else. I stand up and lean against the window, looking up at the streetlights lining Main Street. The single traffic light turns from red to green and the empty intersection remains empty.

I shake my head. What was I thinking, coming here? I should have stuck to what I knew and stayed in the city. I wanted to get away from New York, I wanted to try something new and now I'm starting to feel at home in this town. How the fuck did that happen?

When I first got here everyone seemed like a redneck. Things moved slowly and I didn't understand it. Now it seems almost comforting. Things are always where I expect them to be, and small niceties become an everyday occurrence.

It's like Jess's grandmother. She taught me more about plants and gardening in a couple hours than I'd learned in my whole life.

I sigh and move away from the window, lying back in bed.

Tomorrow is a new day. Maybe I'll bring Jess's grandmother some flowers from the garden tomorrow, as a thank you for teaching me so much. Maybe Jess will be there, and I'll be able to see those eyes again.

Small niceties. I'm learning things I never expected in this town.

12

JESS

Gram is humming in the kitchen, and I can hear the unmistakable sound of her busy at work. From the smell of it, she's baking something.

I push the door open and rub the sleep out of my eyes.

"Morning, Gram. Any coffee ready?"

"In the pot, honey."

I pour myself a mug and lean on the counter as I watch her work. "Cookies? You trying to fatten me up, Gram?"

She chuckles. "They're not for you, Jessica. I was thinking you could bring them over to Mr. McAllister later, as a thank you for driving us back yesterday."

"Sure, that's nice of you." My heart skips a beat when I think of Owen and what happened in this kitchen last night.

Gram makes a noise to agree and keeps working. I sip on my coffee and look out at the sun shining. Sure beats the weather in New York right now.

I leave my grandmother to her work and head upstairs to get my running clothes on. The whisper of Owen's lips is still on mine and I need to clear my head if I'm going to see him again.

We can't do that. We can't get involved. For one, I'm leaving in a week. And plus, the last thing I want is to leave with more rumors swirling about me. All people seem to do around here is talk and talk and talk. I'd like to be able to come back without having to hide out at Gram's house, for once.

I slip out the front door and head to my favorite trail by the river. I can run for miles without crossing another soul here, just surrounded by forest and water. I used to run and run and run out here, whenever things got too much. It's the perfect therapy.

Today, it feels tough. Every step is a struggle until I find my groove and make it to the shady part of the run. The path winds through the trees and I jump over roots and rocks as I run alongside the river.

My body starts to relax for the first time since the kiss. I take deep breaths and finally hit my stride. I smile, taking a deep breath of fresh air as I run through the woods. I fill my lungs with clean air and breathe out, feeling my muscles scream and then relax into the run. This is my favorite part of a run—when everything seems to fall into place and I feel like I'm flying through the air.

My mind clears and I let my feet take me wherever they will. Before I know it, I've rounded the last corner of the trail and am coming back into town.

I smile and take a deep breath. My legs feel like jelly and my heart is pumping hard, but I feel good. I needed that. All the tension is gone from my system and after a shower and some food I'll be ready to go see Owen. I'll try to look a bit more put together than the last couple times I've seen him.

I run up to the front porch, hop up the steps and open the door.

"Hey Gram!" I call out into the house. I'm still panting and the sweat is pouring off me. I need water.

"In here!" She says from the kitchen. I wipe the sweat off my forehead and head down the hallway toward her voice. Is she talking to me?

Then another voice speaks and my eyes widen. I push the kitchen door open and there he is.

Owen McAllister.

He's sitting in the same seat he was in last night, drinking a cup of coffee and eating one of Gram's fresh baked cookies. All of a sudden, the relaxation that I felt disappears and my body tenses. So much for looking put together. I'm a sweaty, red-faced mess and I'm sure my hair is sticking up in every direction. *Great*.

"Jess!" He says as his eyebrows shoot up. A cookie crumb falls off his lip onto his pants and he brushes it off.

"Owen! What are you doing here?"

"Jessica! What a thing to say," Gram says as she shakes her head. "Mr. McAllister brought us these flowers as a thank you. Isn't that nice?"

"It is. Good thing you had those cookies ready or else you'd need to make double as another thank you," I say with a grin as I head to the sink for some water.

Owen laughs and Gram makes a tsk sound.

"These are delicious," he says. "And I don't suppose there's any use in asking you to call me Owen?"

"Probably not," I say with a laugh. His eyes flick over to me and he looks at me from head to toe before clearing his throat and turning to Gram. I turn to the sink again and take a deep breath. Every time he looks at me it sets my body on fire. I was already red-faced from the run and now I must look like I'm about to explode. I take a long drink of water and a deep breath before turning around.

"I'm going to jump in the shower," I say without looking at Owen. I shuffle out of the room and let out a sigh as soon as I turn the corner. My heart is beating faster than it was during my run.

So much for being cool and collected.

13

OWEN

"You're too nice, Mrs. Lee, really."

"Oh it's nothing. I don't need any of this anyways," she replies. I look at the stack of spades, shovels, buckets, fertilizer and I shake my head. It would cost me a fortune to buy this stuff new.

"This will help so much. I only had the one shovel and it's falling apart."

"Take it. I'm too old to garden now," she says as she brushes her hand over an overgrown shrub. She smiles sadly and sighs.

"Would you like me to trim those for you?"

"Oh, that would be lovely!" She says and her eyes light up. "Would you mind?"

"Not at all. Here," I say as I pick up a pair of shears. Jess's grandmother smiles and I see the same light in her eyes as Jess's. She points to a few plants and shows me what needs to be trimmed. I nod and she smiles again and pats my arm.

"You're a dear," she says. I get to work as she heads inside.

I like gardening. It's messy and it's hard work in the hot

sun, but it feels good to do something productive. I'm focused on the shrub when I hear a soft chuckle.

"She put you to work, did she?"

I look up and grin, wiping the sweat off my brow. Jess looks incredible in her sheer blue dress. It's flowing around her legs like water and I blink a few times.

"I offered," I respond with a laugh.

"She made you think you did, anyways," Jess laughs, stepping closer to me and leaning against the porch pillar. "She's an expert at making people feel useful."

"I don't mind," I say, chopping another overgrown branch. "She's helped me so much with the garden at the Lex, and she's offered to give me all this stuff. It's the least I can do."

I glance at her again and remember how she looked in the kitchen, in those skin-tight shorts and sports bra, glistening with sweat. Her hair is down now, falling in soft brown curls around her face. She tilts her head to the side and watches me as I watch her.

"Thank you," she says. Somehow it sounds like she means something more than just gardening. I look at her and she continues. "For helping her. She's on her own out here, I can't tell you how much it means to me. It's nice to know that people are looking out for her."

"It's my pleasure," I answer. I mean it, too. Even just standing here next to Jess is more comfortable and pleasant than I've felt in a long time. She smiles and turns to head back inside.

"I'll help you carry all that stuff back to the hotel, if you want? Did you walk?"

"Sure," I say, and my heart jumps. She smiles at me and turns to go back inside. I chop the shrub and grin to myself, stealing another glance at the door where Jess disappeared.

. . .

Jess and I walk in silence for the first few minutes. It's a comfortable silence, the two of us side by side as we meander through the town. Finally, I turn my head to look at her. The sun is shining off her face and it makes her skin look like it's glowing. She turns to look at me and her pink lips curl up into a smile.

"What?" She asks with a grin.

"Nothing," I respond, turning my head back forward. "So why did you leave?"

Jess laughs and I glance at her again. "You mean why did I leave this Mecca of culture and activity?"

I grin. "I meant more like you sounded bitter when you talked about it. It sounded like there was a reason that you left."

Her smile fades. "People are cruel," she says. I expect her to go on, but she doesn't. She just sighs. "What about you? Why did you leave New York?"

I shrug. I want to tell her about the trial, about the files buried deep in my bottom drawer, about the realization that my dad wasn't the superhero I thought he was. I want to tell her that I left because it was either staying and getting wrapped up in something illegal or leaving and trying to make something of myself.

"I just wanted a change," I finally say. "Everything was moving too fast. It was too loud. I heard about this place and it seemed like something different."

"And now?" She asks, glancing at me. "You still glad you left?"

"You know, if you'd have asked me that a month ago, I would have said no. I would have said I missed the hustle and bustle of the city, that I missed the action. I would have told you I'd be going back the first chance I got. Now I'm not so sure."

She nods but says nothing. We walk in silence for a few minutes until she speaks again.

"There were rumors about me," she says suddenly. I frown. She glances at me. "Before I left. It was like I was invisible. No one would look at me or speak to me. They can turn on you quick," she says. Her voice is flat and she stares straight ahead.

I clear my throat. "I'm sorry to hear that. What... what happened?"

She shrugs. "It's not important. It's okay. They got over it. I got over it. One day everyone just started talking to me again, like nothing happened. It was like a switch flicked. That's when I decided to leave, it was messing with my head too much. Life went on. I moved away and people forgot about it all."

"I'm sorry," I say again. I want to ask her more, to find out what they were saying about her, find out who was saying it. I don't even know what happened but I can feel the first hints of anger and indignation start curling in my stomach.

"It's not your fault," she says as she glances at me. A grin spreads on her face. "I moved here when I was seven. My grandma took me in and raised me. I think I've always been an outsider and some people just used any excuse they needed to shut me out."

"If you're an outsider then I'm from another planet, I respond. "I don't stand a chance then."

"Probably not," she laughs. Her laugh is light and musical and I can't help but chuckle. She glances at me and tilts her head. "You're tall and handsome and you're playing by the rules, so I think you'll be okay."

"Well, thanks for the vote of confidence," I say. She smiles.

"Somehow I feel like I can trust you."

"You can," I reply. Her smile widens. We turn the last corner and the Lex comes into view. We walk the rest of the way in silence and I try to ignore the thumping of my heart in my chest.

14

JESS

I drop the bag of gardening tools on the floor of the shed behind the Lex as Owen leans the shovel and spade against the wall. I brush my hands together and put them on my hips.

"Well that should keep you going for a while."

"Thanks for your help," he says. He turns toward me and his eyes bore into me. My heart jumps and the blood starts rushing in my ears. Every time he's near me he makes me feel dizzy. I don't want to leave, not yet. Owen runs his fingers through his hair.

"You want a drink? Some water? I can show you the renovations we've done on the hotel." He shifts his weight from foot to foot and glances at me. He chews his lip and then his tongue darts out to lick them again.

I nod. "Sure."

The smile spreads on his face and he nods back, gesturing at the shed door. I turn around and shiver as his hand touches the small of my back to guide me out. I lean into his touch and take a deep breath to steady myself.

We walk in silence and go in through the back door. The

hotel is quiet, and our footsteps echo down the long hallway from the back of the hotel toward the lobby.

"Not very busy today," I say. My voice almost trembles and I try to get control over my body again. His hand drops away from the small of my back and I feel more relaxed and more alone all at once.

"No, it's Joe's day off so I've closed the bar till this evening. Not many guests this time of year."

"Are there many guests any time of year?" I laugh. Owen grins but says nothing.

We walk shoulder to shoulder and I breathe in deeply. I can just smell his cologne over the smell of fresh paint in the hotel. I wish I could get closer and bury my head in his chest and run my fingers up his sides. I close my eyes for a moment to try to get a hold over myself again.

Owen starts pointing out architectural features and decisions they made and how long things took to build, but I don't hear a word of it. All I can see is his jaw, and the way the sinews in his neck move when he talks, and the way the muscles in his shoulders and arms ripple under his skin when he moves. He lifts his hand to run his fingers through his hair and I can't help but stare at the little strip of skin between his pants and his shirt.

He hands me a bottle of water from behind the bar. "We've done a lot of work upstairs as well."

"Lead the way," I say with a smile. "The place looks amazing."

"Thanks. It's been a lot of work."

He climbs the stairs two at a time and I try to keep up. He turns around at the top and holds out his hand. I slip my palm into his and an electric current passes from him to me. He smiles, and his eyes darken as his pupils expand. Another thrill passes through my body and I feel like my whole body is warming up. I walk up the last few steps and he keeps a hold on my hand, guiding me down the hallway and showing me the renovations that have been done on the rooms.

We walk all the way to the end of the hall and I glance out the big window. Main Street is buzzing with activity below us. I look up at Owen as he stares out the window and I take a step toward him. My hands rest on his chest and I can feel his heart beating. He turns his head to look at me and wraps his arms around my waist.

My fingers slide up his chest and hook around his neck. Now I can breathe in deeply and let his smell fill my nostrils. I study every detail of his face and run my fingers through the hair at the nape of his neck. His hands drift down from my waist to my back and over my ass. He pulls me into him and I press my body against his.

We say nothing, because nothing needs to be said. His head dips down and finally, finally, I get to taste his kiss again.

15

OWEN

The moment my lips touch hers my whole body gets a few degrees hotter. I wrap my arms around her and pull her closer. I love the way she fits so perfectly against me. Every curve of hers finds just the right place and our bodies connect as if they were made for each other.

Her lips are soft and moist and they taste exquisite. We stand there in the hallway, arms wrapped around each other for seconds or minutes or days—I don't know. Time loses all meaning. My fingers trail down her back and I sink my fingers into her body. She purrs and my cock pulses between us.

Ever since she appeared in her grandmother's kitchen after her run, my whole body has been on edge. All I've wanted to do is grab her and pull her into me, run my fingers all over her body and explore every inch of her.

When she appeared on the porch wearing that blue dress, I could hardly stand straight. When we walked back together it was the sweetest torture to be that close to her. When she slipped her fingers into mine it was like the volume in the world got turned up a couple notches.

And now, now, she's wrapped around me. Her lips are crushed against mine and her hand is fisted into my hair. She pulls at my hair and the tiny needles of pain penetrate my skull and make my cock leap in my pants.

She makes that purring sound again and presses herself closer to me, so that my cock is pinned between us. I groan.

"You're incredibly sexy," I growl as I touch my forehead to hers.

Her eyes are closed and a grin floats over her lips. She pulls her head away and strokes my cheek with her finger.

"I could say the same about you," she finally replies.

We stare at each other for a few moments. I never knew that two people could say so much without ever speaking a word. Her eyes are deep pools of brown, telling me a thousand things while she says nothing. I feel my lips pull into a smile and I nod my head at my door.

"Let's go in here," I say. She smiles and lets me lead the way to the room. I pull out my keys and step through to my room. The bed isn't made and yesterday's clothes are in a pile on the floor. I cringe as I close the door behind her.

"Well that was a convenient place to end the tour," she says with a grin as she swings her eyes over to me. "We just happened to be right beside your room."

I chuckle. "The tour wasn't over. If I remember correctly it was *you* who kissed *me* out there."

Her smile widens and her eyebrow lifts. "Is that so?"

She takes a step toward me and my heart starts hammering against my chest. This time, I don't know who kisses who. Our arms wrap themselves around the other's body and our lips find each other in an instant.

I squeeze my arms around her and let my hands drop over her ass. I pull her into me and she moans again, tangling her fingers into my hair.

Her dress bunches in my hands and I pull the fabric up until my hands are touching her bare skin. The instant my hands touch her skin my whole body feels electrified. My cock throbs in between us and she moves her hips back and forth.

She's not close enough. I want more. I reach down and pick her up by the thighs. She yelps and giggles and then wraps her legs around my waist, letting her arms rest on my shoulders. She kisses my lips gently, slowly, and I let my hands slide over her soft skin. I back up until my legs hit the bed and then I sit down.

Her legs are straddling me and she grinds her hips against me slowly at first, and then more and more insistently. I groan, and she pulls away and smiles.

"This isn't what I was expecting to happen when I offered to help you bring those tools back."

"Isn't it?" I ask with a raised eyebrow.

She laughs. "I was just being neighborly!"

"Neighborly," I repeat with a laugh. "What kind of neighborhood do you live in?" She laughs and I kiss her neck, tracing it all the way down to her collarbone. "I think this was your plan all along. The garden tools were just a distraction. You're a temptress and you've caught me in your web."

"Maybe," she says with a laugh, running her fingers through my hair as my lips follow her collarbone down to her breast. She groans. "Your lips feel so nice."

"I could kiss you forever," I reply, placing a kiss in the center of her chest. I move the soft blue fabric down slightly and see the lacy edge of her bra. I place a kiss just on the edge of it, loving the way her breast is soft under my lips.

She moans and grinds her hips against me as I pull her dress down further. I slip the bra straps off her shoulders and expose more of her skin. I move slowly, caressing her shoulder with my fingertips, and then her chest, and finally trace my fingers along her bra. She reaches back and unclasps her bra, sliding it off and tossing it on the ground.

I groan, moving both my hands to her chest as she wraps her hands around me again. I kiss her again and again and again. I can't get enough of her. Jess's skin tastes incredible. Her nipples are two hard little buds and I pinch them gently between my fingers before taking one in my mouth.

I don't know how we got here, or how it is that I've met a woman like her in a town like this, but right now I don't care about anything except feeling her body against mine.

16

JESS

I'M TREMBLING from just the feeling of his hands on my skin. The way he runs his fingers over and back across my chest and down my spine is making my head spin. It's like every inch of skin that he touches is set on fire, and all I can do is sit here and enjoy the blaze.

With my legs wrapped around his waist, I grind myself into him a little bit harder. He groans, and I feel his cock pulse between us.

I want him so bad. I don't know if I've ever wanted anyone this bad.

The heat in my center is making me dizzy, and with every touch of his fingers and his lips it only grows hotter.

He takes my breast in his lips and I let my head fall backward. I moan as he kisses my nipple and then inhale sharply as he bites it ever so gently. His teeth drag on my skin and the nerve endings in my body start screaming with pleasure.

I run my hands over his shoulders, around his neck, on his chest. Every smooth muscle is rock hard on his body and my hands roam all over. I drop my hand between us, tracing every bump on his chest and abdominal muscles until I find the bulge in his pants. He feels rock hard as I start stroking him gently outside his pants.

He groans and closes his eyes, leaning back slightly as I trace the outline of his cock with my fingertips. His hands drop to my hips and then my ass and he digs his fingers into my skin. I press my hand a tiny bit harder over his crotch and he opens his eyes to look at me.

Owen's eyes are cloudy, but sharp. He looks almost drunk, and his lips fall open and my hand continues to move back and forth over his shaft. A groan rumbles in his throat and he stares at me, not moving an inch as I touch him.

His eyes are magnetic. I can't look away. It's almost animalistic, the way he's looking at me. He leans back ever so slightly and his eyelids droop down as another groan escapes his lips. I see my own desire reflected in his face. I feel my own hunger when I touch his cock. Everything that he wants, I want it too. I want it more.

As if he reads my mind, his hands grip my waist and he lifts me up and flips me onto the bed. I yelp and giggle as my head hits the pillow. Owen turns to me and reaches up my dress until he finds my panties. He holds himself up on his elbow and starts kissing my breast again as his other hand slips under my underwear to find my sopping wet slit.

As soon as he touches it, he groans. He pushes my panties to the side and drags his fingers through my wetness before bringing his hand up to his mouth. He slides his fingers into his mouth and glances up at me as he groans.

"God, that tastes good," he says in a low growl.

The words catch in my throat. I can't say anything. My heart is pounding in my chest and all I can do is watch as he runs his fingers back up the inside of my thigh and slips them smoothly inside me.

My body shudders the second his fingers enter me. My

walls grip him as he starts stroking me, and he moves his lips back to my chest. I tangle my fingers into his hair and moan gently as my body is set on fire.

How does he know how to touch me like this? How does he know which parts of my body are sensitive, where to run his fingertips and where to grip me?

He takes his fingers out of me and gathers the fabric of my dress, pulling it up over my head. It lands next to my bra, but neither of us pay much attention to it. Our eyes are locked on each other, and his hands move down my sides and over my stomach. He shifts his weight so that he's on top of me, covering me with kisses.

Owen explores my body, inch by inch, with his hands first and then with his mouth. He sends pleasure coursing through my veins as every part of my skin is touched and kissed and stroked. He runs his fingers over my underwear and it somehow feels more sensitive than my bare skin. I shudder, and he looks up at me one more time.

"Owen..." I breathe. He groans in reply, dipping his head down to kiss that little crease between my hip and my thigh.

I hook my fingers into my panties and start sliding them down my legs. I kick them off and don't care where they land. My knees fall apart and all I can do is stare at the look on Owen's face.

He scans my body, his eyes half-closed and his lips slightly open. A growl rumbles inside him and my heart pounds against my ribcage. He stays like that, staring at my naked body until I feel like I'm going to come without him even touching me. Finally, after an eternity, he runs his fingers from the center of my chest down between my breasts and over my belly button until he reaches my mound.

This time, when his fingers touch my slit, he doesn't slip them inside. Instead he moves them in slow circles around my bud and I can't help but whimper as he touches me, first softly and then faster as my hips start to buck under his touch.

It's almost too much. I'm dizzy. I can't see straight. The pleasure coursing through my veins is overwhelming as his hands move like magic over me. I can't tell what his hands are doing and what his mouth is doing, my whole body just feels like one wave of pleasure.

Before I know what's happening, my body arches and the pressure inside me explodes. I'm flying over the edge as Owen's hands push me further and further into my pleasure. I whimper and moan until my moans turn to gasps, my body convulsing and my hands gripping the sheets.

I hold on for dear life as my body quivers under his touch. When I can finally move again, I open my eyes and slowly focus them on him. Owen's grinning, still stroking me ever so gently.

"You're so fucking sexy," he growls.

17

OWEN

Watching Jess come is one of the most erotic things I've ever seen. I can't stop watching as she trembles and convulses in front of me. Finally she puts a hand to her brow and sighs.

"Whoa," she manages to say. I grin again.

"Did you enjoy that?"

"Not at all," she replies with a smile. "It was awful."

She spreads her arms and I lay down beside her, trailing my fingers over her body.

"You're still wearing pants," she says softly. "Why are you still wearing pants?" Her eyes search my face and they gleam with mischief. I grin.

"My mistake."

In a couple seconds I'm kicking my pants off the bed and Jess's hand is over my crotch. My cock is straining against my underwear and Jess groans when her hand strokes along my shaft.

"Looks like you enjoyed that almost as much as I did," she says.

"Almost," I manage to reply before she slips her hand under my waistband. The second her hand touches my cock I feel like I'm going to come right here and now. She touches me softly, barely brushing her hand against me but it feels more sensitive than I've ever felt it. I moan and hook my fingers into my underwear, sliding it down my legs and kicking it off to join my pants on the floor.

Jess giggles and grabs my cock in her hand. She makes a small gasp as it throbs against her touch and all I can do is lay my head back and close my eyes.

There's no use with me trying to fight it. I know I'm going to come way too quickly. Even just having her beside me and running my hands along her body is taking me there. Now, with her soft hand stroking up and down my shaft I know I don't stand a chance.

Jess shifts her weight and straddles my leg, all the while stroking me. She brings her lips to mine and I wrap my arms around her, running my fingers through her hair and inhaling her soft perfume. My cock is so hard it almost hurts. It throbs against her hand and she grips it a bit tighter. I groan.

"Do you have a condom?" She asks softly. I say nothing for a second, just staring at her eyes and wondering how I got so lucky. I nod.

It's a flurry of activity to shift my weight and find the box of condoms in my nightstand. I pull one out and look at the little square package. I bought that box ages ago, back when I was in New York. Haven't had much use for these lately. My hands are shaking as I stand and try to tear the crinkling package open. Jess reaches over to keep stroking my cock and my head falls back as I groan.

"That feels too good," I growl.

She laughs softly. "I didn't know it was possible to feel too good."

"It is possible, and this is what it feels like."

I can't take it anymore. I roll the latex over my shaft and Jess lays down on her back. She's looking at me through half-closed eyes and I drag my fingers through her slit. She moans and shivers at my touch before letting her knees fall open.

It's impossible to describe the feeling of entering her. If I thought her hand felt good, I didn't know what I was in for. It's like my cock was made for her, it slides in inch by inch until our bodies are completely connected. I groan as I lean forward, and Jess wraps her legs around my waist. Her fingers wrap around the nape of my neck and she bites her lip.

"You're the sexiest woman I've ever seen," I groan as I drag my hips back and forth. She smiles before her mouth falls open with a small gasp as I push myself deeper inside her.

It's ecstasy. Her walls grip me and her fingers sink into my skin. Her mouth tastes sweet and hot and her body feels impossibly soft under my touch.

She responds to every move I make and our bodies move in sync. We grind and buck and thrust together until our bodies are sweaty and my mind is completely empty. Nothing exists except the pleasure in the pit of my stomach, growing hotter and heavier by the second.

My thrusts get harder and her moans get louder. She grabs my body and I watch her face transform as the pleasure courses through her.

I thought watching her come as I touched her with my hands was erotic. Feeling her come with my cock inside her is indescribable. I can feel every contraction of her muscles, every quiver, every moan that vibrates through her chest. I can feel everything, until everything becomes too much and I'm flying through space with her.

Our bodies are tangled and intertwined as our desire turns to pure passion. She grabs onto me and I soak in every second of pleasure that passes between us as we hold onto each other for dear life.

It's not until the tension subsides and our bodies relax that I pull myself off her, wiping my forehead as the sweat starts to bead.

"Whoa," she says and I grin.

"You seem to be saying that a lot today."

She laughs. "Can't help it."

I lean forward and place a soft kiss on her lips. My heart is still beating fast and I stare deep into her hazel eyes. I can't believe how lucky I am right now.

18

JESS

"Ahh, shit," Owen says as he looks down. "Hold on, let me get you a towel. The condom slipped off when I came out. One sec."

He jumps up, holding the used condom in his hand to throw out. He grabs a towel from the chair and tosses it over to me. It lands directly on my face.

"Thanks," I say as I pull the towel down and glance at him sideways. "Very gentlemanly."

He laughs. "Sorry. I thought speed was more important than gallantry."

I grin and start cleaning up with the towel. "Messy!"

"That's half the fun," he replies with a laugh.

He disappears into the bathroom and comes out a few moments later, crouching down to open the room's mini fridge. He comes and sits on the edge of the bed, hands me a bottle of water and places a carton of strawberries on the bed between us.

"How's that for gallantry," he says with a grin.

I laugh and take a drink of water before handing him the bottle. "It's not bad, I'll give you that. You're a quick learner."

"Are you training me now?" He asks as he bites into a strawberry. "That didn't take long. We only just met the other day."

"Start them early, it's the only way. Like a puppy, you know?" I pop a strawberry into my mouth and smile as he laughs.

He leans down and places a soft kiss on my lips. He sits back up and stares at my face before letting his eyes roam down my body. He shakes his head.

"You're beautiful."

My heart starts beating a bit harder as his eyes flick back up to mine. I smile, suddenly shy. "Not bad yourself," I respond.

He leans down to kiss me again before taking another strawberry in his mouth. I watch as his lips surround the fruit and he bites down into its soft flesh. His jaw flexes as he bites and he makes a small noise in satisfaction.

My phone rings, interrupting our quiet moment. I get up and try to find it through my things strewn all over the room. As soon as it's in my hand I see Sam's name on the screen.

"Oh shit! I was supposed to meet Sam half an hour ago." I pick up. "Hey, Sam! I'm on my way."

"You okay? It's not like you to be late."

I glance at Owen and stifle a laugh. "Yeah, I'm fine. I'm great, actually. Just had to help Gram with some stuff. I'm in town so I'll be at your place in five. Okay, yep. See you."

I hang up the phone and look at Owen, who's laid back in the bed to watch me. He has a grin playing over his lips. "Didn't mean to make you late," he says with a grin. "Sorry about that."

"You're not sorry at all," I say with a laugh. I walk over to the bed and sit on the edge before draping my arm over his chest. "I'll allow it, but only because I've just had two of the most mind-blowing orgasms of my life."

He chuckles as his eyebrows shoot up. I kiss his lips softly and then stand up. "But right now I need to go meet my friend for lunch. She said she had some news for me."

I turn and start gathering my clothes all over the floor, sifting through it to find my underwear. I pull the panties on and pick up my bra.

"When can I see you again?" Owen asks, watching me as I dress.

I shrug. "Tonight?"

A smile spreads across his face and he nods. "Tonight sounds good. The band is playing at the bar again so it should be a good evening."

"Great. We'll be all over each other and start a whole mess of rumors. Give these people something to talk about," I laugh.

"Would that bother you?" He asks. I glance at him and see the seriousness in his question. His eyes aren't playful, he's staring at me curiously. I pause before slipping my dress over my head, chewing on his question.

"No," I finally respond. "It wouldn't bother me, but I'm leaving in a week. You should be the one thinking about the consequences of that kind of chatter."

He just nods and stretches his arms overhead before interlinking them behind his head. He grins as I pull on my dress and fix my hair in the mirror. "I think I can handle a few rumors if it means I get to see you again."

I laugh and walk over to him, kissing him one last time. "Be careful what you wish for," I say with a wink. "I'll see you tonight."

"See you tonight," he replies. I grab my purse and walk to the door, turning one last time to look at him as he lies on his bed. We just smile at each other before I slip out the door and close it softly behind me.

It takes me a second to pull myself together once I'm out of the room. I take a deep breath and smooth my hair down again. I glance at the closed door and a grin pulls at my lips. There's a lightness in my step as I make my way downstairs and out of the hotel.

19

OWEN

Joe is sweeping the front entrance by the time I get downstairs. He glances at me as I pass through the double doors to join him outside

"Late morning?"

I shake my head but I can't think of an excuse, so I just change the subject. "You ready for a big crowd tonight?"

"I was thinking, Owen, it might do us good to hire someone else. I'm not used to having this many people in the bar.

I nod. "You're right. I've been asking too much of you. I'll put out the word. You got anyone in mind?"

"I'll ask around," he replies, shaking his head. Before I can answer, a familiar voice pipes up from the sidewalk.

"Excuse me, I couldn't help but overhear," the voice calls out. I turn to see Mary Hanson's long blonde hair and telltale smirk staring up at me. "Are you hiring?"

"Well, I..." I'm not sure why I'm hesitating. Mary tilts her head to the side.

"I've got experience behind the bar, and I know pretty

much everyone in this town. With the wedding coming up I could use some extra cash."

I turn to Joe who shrugs and goes back to his broom. Mary is still standing there, hip sticking out and taping her foot gently on the pavement. I nod slowly and gulp.

"Well, sure. I can give you a two-week trial period, how does that sound?"

"Sounds great," she says, climbing the three steps to join me on the porch. She sways her hips as she walks toward me and stands a little bit too close to me. She smiles up at me through her lashes. "I won't disappoint you."

I clear my throat and nod. "Okay. Come back around 4 p.m. and Joe will show you where everything is. Won't you, Joe?"

Joe grunts in response and I nod again. I take a step to the side and jump down the stairs onto the sidewalk. Mary's eyes follow me the whole way and when I look back at her, she's still got that smirk on her face. She flicks her hair behind her shoulder and smiles a bit wider.

I nod my head quickly and turn to the back of the building. On paper, it seems great to hire some extra help. But Mary Hanson? I'm not sure why I have a bad feeling about this. I shake my head to get rid of the feeling and clear my head.

The sun is shining and people are out. I head out back to the shed to start working on some of these flowerbeds with my new garden tools. As soon as I step into the shed and see those tools I think of Jess, and the hours that just went by. I can't help whistling to myself as I grab a spade and a pair of garden shears. By the time I'm back at the front of the Lex, there's a smile plastered over my face. I never thought I'd have Jess in my bed today, and I definitely didn't think that I'd have plans to see her again tonight.

I mean, I didn't think I'd have any woman in my bed while I was in this town, let alone a woman as gorgeous and smart as she is. I think of the way she grins, or how she always has a quick remark. She's made me laugh more in one day than anyone else has made me laugh in months.

It feels *good* to be with her. Surprisingly good.

It feels good to be close to a woman—no—to be close to *her*. It feels good to know that I'll see her again tonight, and hopefully every night until she leaves.

These thoughts creep up on me and I shake my head. Am I getting attached? I shouldn't be, it's not like me and plus, it's only been a day. I know she's leaving in a week but that doesn't mean I can't enjoy our time together until then, does it? And then she'll be gone and I'll be back to business as usual.

It's almost better that she's leaving.

Yeah, it's better!

This way I'm forced to not get attached. We can just have mind-blowing sex until she leaves and then we'll say our goodbyes. By the time she's back in town, whenever that is, I'll have sold the hotel off and moved on.

I shove the spade into the rich brown earth along the front of the building and can't help but feel that it won't be that easy to forget about her.

20

JESS

I practically float down the stairs and out the door. The sun is blinding and I squint for a few moments until my eyes adjust. I turn toward Sam's house and smile as the warmth of the sun soaks into my skin. A bird sings nearby and I sigh in contentment.

That was... unexpected. Unexpectedly great, actually. Definitely not what I thought I'd experience when I came back home. I think of my friends in New York and I can't wait to tell them all about it. I'll have to find a photo of Owen so I can show them what he looks like.

I grin as I think about it and almost bump into Mary Hanson as she walks down the sidewalk.

"In a hurry?" She asks in that sickly sweet voice of hers. I try not to roll my eyes.

"Always. It's the big city thing, you know?"

"You never were one for waiting," she says with an eyebrow raised. I bristle, trying to hold back the wave of memories that's waiting to burst through my mind. She smiles but her eyes stay blank and she continues. "What were you doing at the Lex?"

"What?"

"The Lex. You just walked out. What were you doing?"

She leans on every word and I take a deep breath. I forgot how careful I had to be around this town. I paint a similar smile on my own face.

"Gram gave Mr. McAllister some old garden tools and I was just delivering them."

"You're pretty happy to be delivering some garden tools," she shoots back.

"Just glad to be home, Mary," I respond. "Excuse me."

I step around her and keep walking without looking back. I can feel her eyes on the back of my head and I force myself to keep walking forward. She may have had power over me when I was sixteen, but she doesn't have any now. I'm my own woman and I've been through worse than being the subject of her wagging tongue.

By the time I get to Sam's house, I've forgotten about Mary. I ring the doorbell and Sam answers within a second. She steps out to give me a hug.

"Gorgeous as usual," she says with a smile. She tucks a strand of hair behind her ear and smiles. "Leave some for the rest of us."

"Oh stop it, Sam. You know you're a knockout," I answer with a laugh. She shrugs and another voice pipes up behind her.

"She sure is," the deep baritone voice says. A head pops around the corner and our childhood friend, Ronnie, appears in the doorway.

"Ronnie!" I say. "I thought you'd moved to Philadelphia!"

"I'm back," he says simply. He and Sam exchange a glance and—did she just blush? He reaches over to give me a hug and Sam ushers us inside. We sit down in the living room and Sam brings us some water.

"Thanks," I say as she hands me one and then moves to sit next to Ronnie on the couch. He puts his hand around the back of the sofa and looks at Sam with that same look again. I swallow. "So... what was the big news that you wanted to tell me about?"

There it is—that look again. Ronnie and Sam glance at each other and then at me.

"We're getting married," Sam says simply. She shrugs and then a smile spreads across her face.

"What?" I answer. I'm still confused. "To each other?"

Ronnie laughs. "Yes, to each other. God, Jess, for such a genius you can be pretty slow."

"But... how... when?" I know I should be happy for them but somehow, I can't let myself feel good for them. It seems like everyone in my life is getting married and having children and I'm still single. Both my best friends in New York, Harper and Rosie, are all loved up with kids and now Sam too? I'm still having casual sex with men I've just met.

Suddenly I'm not so excited to tell my friends about my escapades.

Sam smiles again. "Ronnie came back last year and I don't know, it just... happened."

"Wow," I say.

Sam frowns. "Are you... are you okay? Are you happy for us?"

I snap back to myself and smile. "Of course I'm happy for you," I say. I stand up and give Sam a hug. "Of course I'm happy for you. Congratulations." I turn to Ronnie and give him a hug too. "So all those times you were putting worms down our shirts it was just a long con to bag Sam, was it?"

Ronnie laughs. "Something like that." They exchange another look and I feel a pang of jealousy in my chest.

"So why didn't you tell me? I've spoken to you since

Ronnie got back, you never even mentioned you were dating."

Sam wrings her hands. "I didn't know how to tell you. I don't know. You were in New York and I didn't think that you'd really care what was going on in this small town. And then Ronnie asked me last week and I thought I'd tell you in person."

I wince and I can feel my heart cracking. I try to think of the last time I spoke to Sam and I can't even remember. "Sam," I say slowly. "Ronnie..."

My voice trails off and Sam looks at me with tears in her eyes. I swallow and speak again. "I am over the moon for you guys. We should celebrate tonight!"

Sam grins. "The band is back at the Lex tonight. Ma has the nurse over so I'm free to get away."

"Perfect," I say. "The Lex it is."

The two of them are on the sofa and Ronnie puts his hand over her shoulder. She leans into him and I feel that pang of jealousy again.

I want that.

I sit back down and take a sip of water as I watch them and I think it again: I want that. I want to be happy with someone, and feel completely comfortable with them and look forward to sharing my life with them.

Instead, what do I have? I have sex with the new hotel owner that I only met a couple days ago.

Sure, it was incredibly hot sex, and the thought of seeing him again makes my heart jump, but it wasn't *this*. It wasn't Sam and Ronnie, knowing each other their whole lives and looking forward to spending the rest of it together. Ronnie leans over and kisses Sam on the temple and my heart squeezes again. I never thought I'd feel like the third wheel with my two oldest friends.

Sam looks at me again and opens her mouth. It takes a few moments for her to speak. "Jess, there was something else I wanted to ask you."

"Yeah?"

"Would you," she pauses. "Would you be my maid of honor?"

The tears start welling up in my eyes immediately and I jump up. I run over to the both of them and wrap my arms around Sam.

"Of course, I'd be honored. Oh, Sam…"

The two of us have tears streaming down our faces and we hurry to brush them away. "So when's the date? Have you guys decided?"

"It's this summer," Sam says with a huge smile. "July 4th. Oh, please tell me you can make it!"

"July 4th! This year! But that's only two months away! You're not…" I touch my hand to my stomach and they both laugh.

"Nope. Just don't see the sense in waiting." She turns to Ronnie and they kiss each other sweetly. The jealousy inside me evaporates and I can't help but feel happy for the two of them. They look so happy and so in love.

"Right, you hungry?" Sam asks, putting her hands on her knees to stand up.

"Starving," Ronnie and I both answer at the same time. There's a pause and then the three of us burst out laughing. My chest relaxes and Sam shakes her head. Even though they're getting married, they're still the same as they were when we were seven.

21

OWEN

Mary Hanson can definitely work behind a bar. I'll give her that. She's fast and efficient and works well with Joe next to her. Maybe my uneasy feeling before was just because I don't know her that well, and she has the habit of flirting with everyone. This could be a good fit.

I glance around at the room as it starts filling up and sigh.

She's not here yet.

I check my watch—the band should be starting in half an hour, so the place will be packed in an hour or two. I look at the door again and jump when I hear Mary's voice behind me.

"Waiting for someone?"

"What?" I ask as I turn. "No, why?"

"You're watching that door like the President of the United States is about to walk through," she says with an eyebrow raised.

"Maybe he is," I grin. "You never know."

"Mm," she says.

Just then, Jess walks in. She's with Sam and her boyfriend—I can't remember his name. Jess's eyes scan the room and find me in an instant. My heart starts hammering against my ribs as we stare at each other from across the room.

Mary makes a noise and then puts her hand on my chest. I lean away from her, frowning. She starts laughing and leans into me, pressing her chest into my side.

"Looks like it wasn't the president you were waiting for," she whispers. She laughs again and walks away.

I glance back at Jess and she looks away quickly, turning her back to me as she gestures to a table. The three of them nod and head toward the table and away from me.

Fuck.

I glance back at Mary with acid in my eyes but she ignores me. She opens a bottle of beer and puts it in front of a man at the bar, leaning over to show off her cleavage for him before taking the cash he hands her for the drink.

I shake my head and head to Jess's table. I'm not going to let her ignore me like that.

The three of them are laughing at something when I walk up to the table. Sam greets me first.

"Owen! How are you?"

"I'm great Sam, good to see you here."

"Well, I'll be honest, it's the only place in town," she says with a laugh. "Don't know where else we would go."

"I'm Ronnie, nice to meet you. I've heard all kinds of things about you!" Sam's partner says with a loud laugh. I like him already. We shake hands and I turn to Jess.

"Hey, Jess."

My cock throbs as she swings those eyes to mine. Her tongue slides out to lick her lips and she dips her chin down. "Hey."

"You guys want some drinks?" I ask.

"Sure," Sam says, smiling.

Jess nods to the bar. "New barmaid?"

I turn to see Mary looking at us and then face the table again. "Probationary period. Joe said he needed some extra help and Mary overheard us. The locals seem to like her."

Jess just nods. She glances at the bar and her eyes narrow slightly for a moment. She turns to her friends and then claps her hands.

"Well, we are celebrating the engagement of my two oldest and dearest friends, so I think… champagne? What do you guys think?"

Sam laughs and Ronnie nods. "Sounds good."

Jess turns to me, brushing her hand against my leg under the table so no one can see. "Mr. McAllister," she says with a grin. "Bring us a bottle of your finest French Champagne!" She waves with a flourish and then laughs. "Or, you know… some sparkling white wine of some sort. The cheaper the better, I'm not made of money and we won't be able to tell the difference anyways."

I grin. "This one's on the house, guys. Congratulations."

"That's very generous of you, Mr. McAllister," Jess says with a grin.

"Don't you start calling me that," I laugh as I turn away. "It's bad enough that your grandmother refuses to call me by my name."

The three of them laugh and my heart does a flip as I walk toward the bar. I can feel Jess's eyes on me and all I want to do is grab her and wrap her in my arms and never let go.

22

JESS

"What was *that* about?" Sam asks with a raised eyebrow as Owen walks away. I spin my head back to her, hoping she didn't notice me staring at his ass.

"What was what about?" I ask innocently.

"Jess," she says.

"Sam," I respond.

Ronnie laughs. "You guys got the hots for each other or what?"

"No!" I say just a little bit too loud. They both laugh.

"The lady doth protest too much... or whatever," Ronnie says again. "It's okay, Jess. It's not like it was some secret the way you two were eye fucking the shit out of at each other."

"Ronnie!" Sam exclaims. She turns to me and adds: "I was wondering whose engagement we were actually celebrating."

I roll my eyes as I feel my cheeks blush. "Stop it," I laugh. "Fine, fine! He's an attractive guy, what can I say? A girl can look, can't she?"

"Yeah, and a girl does look," Sam says pointedly. I laugh and shrug just as our bottle of sparkling wine appears at the table.

Instead of Owen holding it, it's Mary Hanson. She places the bucket of ice and bottle on the table and puts three glasses down. "I'm told this is on the house," she says, staring at me. A smirk is hiding just behind her lips. "We didn't have any *French Champagne*, so I hope this will do."

"It'll have to," I reply with a shrug.

Sam laughs. "It's perfect. Thanks Mary."

Mary nods. "So you guys engaged, huh?" Sam nods and Mary continues: "Congratulations. Looks like we'll have two weddings in town this year."

"Looks like it, yeah," Sam responds. "When's yours?" She was always better at being polite than I was. My eyes scan the room for Owen and I spot him by the bar, talking to old man Howard. Their conversation is animated and Owen makes a big gesture with his arms over his head and they both laugh. Howard claps him on the back and I smile. He seems to have slipped into the fabric of the town seamlessly. They like him. How could they not?

For some reason the thought of my hometown liking him makes my heart grow a couple sizes in my chest. I look at the smile on Owen's face as he talks with Howard and I can feel my center heating up. He runs his fingers through his hair in that familiar motion of his and my eyes flick down to the strip of exposed skin at his hips.

My mouth gets dry and my mind jumps back to his bed a few hours ago. My fingertips tingle as I think of putting my hands on his skin again, and wrapping my fingers around his thick cock.

"...Jess?"

I turn to Sam, eyebrows up near my hairline. "Yeah? Sorry, I zoned out."

Sam purses her lips but says nothing. "I was just telling Mary that you were my maid of honor for the wedding."

"Right, yeah. I can't wait," I say with a smile, reaching over the table and squeezing Sam's hand.

"Quick engagement," Mary says with a raised eyebrow as she pours the sparkling wine into our glasses. "Not wasting any time. I've been engaged for over a year already!"

"Don't see the point," Sam says. She smiles at Mary who nods with a sour expression on her face. She puts the bottle in the ice bucket and nods before turning back to the bar. I instantly feel more relaxed as she walks away from our table. I turn to my two oldest friends and smile.

The three of us pick up our glasses. "To love, friendship, and weddings," I say solemnly. We clink our glasses together and take a sip. I smile as the bubbles explode on my tongue and hold the glass up in front of me.

"Tastes like French Champagne to me," I say with a grin.

"It's bubbly," Ronnie answers with a shrug and a laugh. "That's all that matters, isn't it?"

Sam and Ronnie turn to each other and exchange another loving kiss. I smile and look away, wanting to give them a second of privacy. My eyes find Owen's. His brown eyes bore into mine from across the room and I wonder what I see in them. Desire, yes, but is there something else?

A smile spreads across my face as we look at each other until Sam and Ronnie start laughing.

"You know this is a hotel, right?" Sam asks. "You guys can get a room. He owns the place so it shouldn't be that hard to organize."

I blush and roll my eyes, throwing my hands up in surrender. "All right, all right, all right," I answer with a laugh. I pick up my glass of bubbly and steal just one more glance at Owen before burying my nose in my drink.

23

OWEN

It's like there's a sensor in my brain that can always detect where Jess is in the room. I can sense when she gets up to go to the bathroom, even though I'm on the other end of the bar. She glances at me and our eyes meet for just a second before we both look away. When she gets up to go get drinks, I feel myself turning toward her.

She's still wearing that sheer blue sundress and it's driving me wild. I steal glances her way whenever I can, and our eyes meet more often than not. All I want to do is go sit next to her, put my arm around her shoulder and spend the whole night listening to her laugh and talk. I don't remember the last time a woman had me this hooked.

"So you in love now or what?" Mary says to me as she leans against the bar across from me. That same smirk is playing on her lips and my head snaps away from Jess and over to her. The smile on her lips doesn't penetrate all the way up to her eyes. Instead, I see something in them I don't recognize. Malice? Or anger?

I shake my head and ignore her question. Old man Howard chuckles beside me.

"I don't blame you," he says. "Jessica Lee has grown into a beautiful young woman. Always smart, too. Do you know that she won a scholarship to Columbia? Graduated with honors," he says, glancing over at Jess. My cheeks start to burn as I realize how obviously I've been staring at her. She looks over and nods at Howard when she sees him looking over.

"A scholarship to Columbia University? In New York?"

"Mm-hmm," Howard says.

I frown. "She never told me that." All she told me was that she moved away to New York as soon as she could.

"She doesn't talk about much, that one. Not about herself, anyway." Howard lifts his beer to his mouth and empties it before pushing it toward Mary on the other side of the bar. "Get me another one, darling."

I look at Mary and see her face completely clouded over. There's a darkness in her eyes as she nods and turns to the fridges full of beer behind her. I frown as I watch her, waiting to see the expression on her face as she turns around to give Howard his beer.

When she does turn around again, her face is completely placid. The anger in her eyes is gone and she has a pleasant smile on her lips. She pops the beer open and places it down in front of the old man. He grunts in thanks.

I almost jump when Jess's hand touches my back. She slides in beside Howard and I, putting her arm around Howard and giving him a kiss on the cheek.

"Howard!" She says. "I haven't seen you in years. How are you? How are the kids?"

Howard smiles at Jess and they exchange pleasantries. I watch the way the dim light in the bar reflects off her hair, making it look like a million different shades of brown. She looks radiant, and she definitely looks like she doesn't belong in a place like this.

I clear my throat. "So Howard was telling me you graduated from Columbia?"

Jess looks over at Howard and he shrugs. "What else have you been saying about me, Howard? Nothing too incriminating, I hope?"

Howard chuckles and shakes his head. Jess smiles and I see a warmth in her as she looks at the old man. He seems to love her, and I don't blame him. There's something about her that just makes her personality magnetic. She turns to me and finally swings her eyes up to mine. The breath catches in my lungs as her gaze focuses on my face and she smiles.

"Yeah, I left for college ten years ago."

"Well it's too bad New York couldn't hold your attention longer," Mary pipes up from behind the bar. She's staring at Jess with fire in her eyes. Jess glances at her and I feel her body stiffen beside me. She stares at Mary for a few moments before speaking.

"Can I get two beers and a vodka soda? Thanks."

Mary bristles and I see the cloud pass over her face again. She opens her mouth and then closes it again before starting to make the drinks. As soon as they're on the bar, Jess gives her some money and nods to Howard and I.

"Excuse me, gentlemen."

"You enjoy yourself," Howard says with a smile. "Good to see you again, Jess."

Jess smiles. "Good to see you too, Howard."

I watch her walk back to her table and desperately want to follow her there, but I keep my feet glued where they are. People have already noticed me looking at her, it would surely cause a riot if they knew I'd had her in my bed a few hours ago.

24

JESS

"I might stay and watch the band a bit longer," I say as Sam and Ronnie stand up to leave. Owen is leaning against the wall, talking to someone else in the back corner of the bar. Sam spreads her arms and gives me a hug.

"Good to see you, Jess. You seem really happy."

"I am. And congratulations again, to both of you."

Ronnie gives me a big bear hug and I watch them walk away, hand in hand. I sit back down at the table and within a few moments, Owen is sliding into the chair across from me.

I grin. "Are you sure you should be doing that," I say with a raised eyebrow. "You're starting rumors already."

"I don't give a shit about rumors," he responds. He's staring at me with half-closed eyes and he leans forward. I lift the drink to my lips and take a sip. When I put it back down, he speaks in a low voice, barely above a whisper. "You've been driving me wild all evening."

"Me?" I answer innocently. My eyebrows shoot up toward my hairline. "What have I done?"

"Swanning around here with that dress and those eyes,"

he answers with a grin. "I can't stop thinking about this afternoon."

"How long do you have to be here?" I ask, taking another sip of my drink.

"I was thinking of going to bed soon," he answers with a grin.

I nod slowly, flicking my eyes to his and trying not to smile. "That's too bad. I thought we could spend some time together this evening. But if you're tired..."

"I could be convinced."

I laugh. "You go first, I'll meet you up there in ten minutes."

"Does it have to be this top secret? Surely no one would care?"

I glance over at the bar and see Mary staring at us. I shrug. "I'm not the one who's living here, you're the one who will have to deal with the fallout."

He shakes his head. "You know these people better than I do. See you in ten."

He stands up and I realize my heart is hammering against my ribcage. I force myself to not stare at him as he walks away, instead looking over at the band. The minutes tick by so slowly it hurts. All I can think about is Owen and how his body felt when I was running my fingers all over it. Now that he's gone, the room feels colder and darker than it did just moments ago.

I glance at my phone again and sigh. I look up my friend Rosie's number.

Jess: You'll never guess what's happening right now.

I put my phone down and sip my drink slowly. Within a couple minutes it buzzes again.

Rosie: ??

I type away quickly and hit send.

Jess: Foxy new hotel owner. May or may not have had the hottest sex of my life this afternoon and may or may not be heading up to see him in a couple minutes.

This time it only takes a couple seconds to buzz in response.

Rosie: 😂😂😂 *You hussy. What about your arch nemesis, is she there? What's her name again? And how's your grandma? You told me your hometown was boring. It sounds better than New York!*

Jess: She's giving me the stink eye as we speak. I respond. *Gram is good, but seems a lot older. Okay got to go, my lover is waiting. Say hi to little Jack and Lucas for me.*

Rosie: Can't wait to hear the details xx

I smile and put my phone away. Rosie just got married to the love of her life, Lucas, after having an unplanned pregnancy with him. Between her and our other friend Harper, I'm the last one to be unmarried and not have any kids. With Sam getting married now it's starting to feel very lonely. Not only am I unmarried, but I don't even have any prospects for a real relationship anywhere on the horizon.

I shake my head and stand up. I might not have any husband prospects on the horizon, but I do have an incredibly sexy man waiting to screw my brains out upstairs.

I walk out the front of the hotel, waving goodbye to Old Man Howard. I turn left and take the long way around the block before glancing around me and darting down the alley behind the Lex. I find the backdoor and slide through, creeping up the back stairwell. I make it to Owen's floor and walk to his door. I lift my hand and knock gently.

Tap-tap-tap.

It only takes a couple seconds for it to swing open. Owen reaches over and grabs me by the waist, pulling me inside and slamming the door behind me. He pulls me close and crushes his lips against mine, tangling his fingers into my hair and dipping me backward. Our kiss is electric, and my whole body feels like it's buzzing. I wrap my arms around him and sink my fingers into any piece of him I can find.

Finally, we come up for air. I brush my hair back and pant as Owen grins.

"What took you so long," he growls, rubbing his nose back and forth against mine. I close my eyes and breathe in deeply, inhaling that spicy cologne and musk that drives me insane anytime he's near.

"I had to take a walk around the block to avoid suspicion," I answer. He laughs and I smile. "I came up the back stairs."

"Are you that embarrassed to be with me?" He asks. There's a pang in my chest at his words and I shake my head.

"I'd show you off to everyone I meet," I answer softly, stroking his cheek with the back of my fingers. I run my hands across his temple and back into his hair and he groans. "You don't know what this town is like," I add. "They can be ruthless."

"They seem pretty nice to me," he says as he places a gentle kiss on my lips.

"It's better this way," I say, staring into his eyes. "Trust me."

He nods but I'm not sure he understands. There's a certain way of doing things around here. He kisses me again and the thoughts evaporate from my head. For now, all that matters are his hands on my body and his kiss against mine.

25

OWEN

ALL THE TENSION inside me explodes at once. I can't get enough of her. I can't touch her enough, or taste her enough, or hold her enough. Somehow our clothes evaporate and she's straddling me on top of the bed. I feel like I'm drunk, even though I've only had two beers tonight. It's just looking at her body that does it to me, and hearing those little moans she makes when my thumb passes over her clit.

Her nails are digging into my shoulders and she's biting her lip. I sink my teeth into her shoulder and grab her closer. I've never met a woman like this. She lets go completely. Her face betrays only complete ecstasy.

This time when I come, it feels like fire burning through my veins. My whole body contracts at once and I lose control. She gasps but it's like it's muffled, I can't hear properly. I can't think and the edges of my vision go blurry and all I can see is her on top of me until the air invades my lungs again and I can breathe.

I can't breathe though, not really, I can only pant. Shallow, jagged breaths drag in and out of my lungs and I can't speak yet. I hear her chuckle softly and I feel the kiss she lays on my cheek, but I can't do anything about it. Not yet. Not until my body comes under my control again and I turn to the side and drape my arm over her body. She sighs and wriggles under my arm as I stroke her back up and down.

"How do you do that," I whisper. She opens her eyes and stares straight at me.

"Do what?"

"That," I answer, dipping my chin down. "What you just did."

She laughs. "Just let go and move my hips, I guess. It's not an exact science." She smiles again and I lean forward to kiss her lips. She makes a little moan and I run my fingers up and down her spine.

"Did you come?" I ask.

Jess smiles. "Not this time, but that's okay."

I shake my head. "It's not okay."

She laughs. "It is okay. Stop worrying."

I trace her cheek with my finger and pinch her earlobe gently before tucking a strand of stray hair behind her ear.

"I like that you're honest about it," I say. She looks at me and frowns slightly, still smiling.

"Honest about what?"

"About not having an orgasm. I like that you didn't fake it."

She laughs and wraps her fingers around my neck, bringing her lips to mine and kissing me more gently than she has before.

"That's one thing you don't have to worry about," she says. "I'm no porn star and I'm definitely never going to fake it."

I grin. "You're not a porn star? You had me fooled with those moves."

She laughs and smacks my shoulder gently. I move quickly, rolling myself onto her as she giggles and yelps, then kissing my way down her body and spreading her legs. My head hovers over her mound and she lets out a sigh.

"You don't have to do that, Owen. I don't need to come every time." I look up at her and see she's looking at me, her hand running gently through my hair.

"I want to do this. It's not some chore to eat you out," I say, kissing the crease between her hip and her leg. "What makes you think I wouldn't want to do this?"

Suddenly she seems embarrassed. "I don't know, I've never been with anyone who... who enjoys that."

I lift my head up and frown. "You... what? You've never been with someone who enjoys going down on you?" She shakes her head slowly and I exhale slowly. "Well, Jess. Ever since the day I met you down at the bar I have been dreaming about tasting your pussy," I growl. Her eyebrows shoot up but she says nothing. Her chest is moving up and down with every breath and I grin as I bring my lips down to her slit.

I wasn't lying. I have wanted to taste her ever since I laid eyes on her. Now, with my head buried between her legs and my tongue exploring her slit I'm finally doing it, and it's better than I could have imagined.

She whimpers as I move my mouth back and forth, and I feel her tremble as my tongue surrounds her bud. I wrap my arms around her legs and I feel her grab my hair in her fist.

"Owen," she breathes. I moan in response. I'm not taking my mouth away, not yet. She tastes too good, and the noises she's making are driving me wild. Her hips start to move with me and I groan again. Her hand fists into my hair and the tiny needles of pain in my skull only make me want her more.

My cock is hard again, but it doesn't matter. My fingers grip her legs as I devour her, and I'm not going to stop until she's screaming my name.

26

JESS

I WAS TELLING the truth when I'd told him that no man had ever enjoyed going down on me. And now, here is the sexiest man I've ever met with his head buried between my legs. The sensations flowing through my body are indescribable. I whimper again and he groans, sending small vibrations running between my legs.

"You taste so good," he growls as he looks up at me. I know my eyes are wide and I'm panting, but I can't think of anything to answer. The fact that he's enjoying this is turning me on more than what he's doing.

He slides a finger inside me and dips his mouth back down to my clit. I gasp. My walls grip down on his finger and I tilt my hips toward his mouth until the ball of heat in my stomach feels like it's about to erupt. He groans again and I grab his head, pushing it down between my legs.

I don't know what he's doing. He's tasting and touching me. I can't tell the difference between his fingers and his mouth. All I feel is pleasure. It doesn't matter because whatever he's doing is enough to send me over the edge. No, it's more than enough, way more than enough. His fingers curl up and find my most sensitive spot and suddenly the heat inside me is spreading at light speed through my body.

"Owen," I gasp, and then cry out. I lose myself and lose my voice and my back arches as the fire fills my veins and spreads through my body. I close my eyes and gasp, gripping his hair as he tastes me and touches me until nothing exists except him, me, and my pleasure.

The world could end and it wouldn't matter, not right now. The earth could open up underneath us and swallow us whole and I wouldn't know what was happening. I let the tidal wave of pleasure crash over me again and again and again until the swell dies down and I can think again.

Owen lifts his head up and smiles at me. His lips are moist and there's a hint of wetness in his stubble.

"Did you enjoy that?"

"Fuck, Owen," I manage to say. I bring a hand to my forehead and hear him chuckle.

"Good."

He stands up and grabs some water, taking a long drink before handing me the bottle.

"Thanks," I say, taking a sip. The cool liquid tastes so good as it fills my parched mouth. I groan in satisfaction. "That's good."

"I know," he says. He climbs over me and lays down on the bed next to me. I cuddle in beside him as he drapes his arm over my body. I groan.

"This is so comfortable. I don't want to leave yet."

"So don't," he says softly. "Stay."

I open my eyes and see him looking at me. He's looking at me softly, and he leans over to kiss my forehead. His hand runs through my hair and he massages my scalp gently for a few moments until I groan.

"What are you doing to me," I groan. "You have me under a spell or something, I can't move."

"Stop trying to fight it," he laughs. "Just stay. Come closer. Sleep. We can have breakfast tomorrow and then you can go back to your grandma's place."

I look at him again and see the sincerity in his eyes. My body is still buzzing from the orgasm and I shift a bit closer to him.

"Okay," I say. "If you insist. But I have to leave early before everyone wakes up and sees me do my walk of shame."

"Deal." I smile at him and he strokes my cheek again. He shifts his head to look at me. "I didn't know you went to Columbia. You said you just left as soon as you could."

I nod. "I got a scholarship. It's the only way I could afford to get out of here, otherwise I don't know what I would have done. Resorted to petty crime, probably."

He laughs that big belly laugh that I'm starting to love. "So your choices were successful intelligent college grad or criminal?"

"Basically," I answer with a shrug and a laugh. He doesn't realize how true that statement is. The pressure in this town when everything happened before I left for college was incredible. I was seventeen, alone, and a pariah. The only thing that kept me from falling into an unending depression was Gram's tough love, and school.

"You're the most intriguing woman I've ever met," Owen says as he lifts his head into his palm, looking me up and down. "You're incredibly intelligent and beautiful and resourceful, and you've made something of yourself. Why does this town scare you so much? Why are you so afraid of what people think? It doesn't make sense."

I sigh. How can I explain it? How can I explain the torture I went through as a teenager? Trying to keep Mary Hanson and her gang of bullies away from me while being better at her in school and having a boyfriend before her? I know she liked him, and sometimes I wonder if that's what started it all off. Just plain old teenage jealousy that snowballed into psychological warfare between the two of us.

"They just turn on you quickly around here," I finally say. "It's easier to just stay out of the headlines."

He grunts in response and nods. "You can say that again."

"You're lucky I'm only here for a couple more days," I say with a grin. "It's the only redeeming thing about this whole situation."

"Doesn't feel like luck," he says gently. I open my mouth to answer but can't think of anything. Owen wraps his arm around me and I put my head on his chest. He kisses the top of my head and I fall into a deep, peaceful sleep.

27

OWEN

I FEEL like the luckiest man alive. I wake up as the sun is streaming through the window and look over to see Jess snoring softly on the pillow beside me. I still haven't bought any blinds, but this morning it doesn't seem to bother me. We're both still completely naked, and I run my fingers down her side and over her hip.

I sigh as I feel the curves of her body. She shifts and groans as her eyes flutter open.

"Morning," she says.

"Morning."

She rolls onto her back and stretches her arms overhead, groaning in satisfaction. "I slept so well," she says. "Better than I've slept in months."

"Orgasms do that to a person," I reply with a chuckle.

She laughs and then glances at the window. Her smile fades and she sits up. "What time is it?"

"I'm not sure. Relax," I say. "It's okay."

"It's definitely not okay," she says, jumping up and flipping over her phone. "Fuck! Shit! It's almost 9am!"

She hurries to the bathroom and when she comes out her

hair is brushed and her face is washed. She pulls on her clothes and I sit up in bed.

"Relax, Jess. Come on," I say, holding out my hands.

She shakes her head. "I have to go. Owen," she says, placing both hands on my shoulders. "You should listen to me. People don't like change around here. People don't like *me* around here. You're playing with fire."

"That doesn't make any sense. I see how people talk to you! Howard seemed to love you! And Sam and her fiancé... No one hates you."

"Howard likes me because he likes my grandmother. The other two are my only friends. People like Mary Hanson have more pull than you realize around here. She can cause a lot of damage..." She trails off and turns around, picking up her dress off the floor. She pulls on her dress and sighs. "Thank you for a great night."

I stand up and wrap my arms around her. "Don't worry about Mary Hanson. She's probably just jealous because you're beautiful and intelligent and funny, and she's not."

Jess smiles softly. "You're playing with fire," she repeats as she lays a gentle kiss on my lips. "Don't say I didn't warn you."

"That doesn't make me want you any less."

"It's not supposed to," she answers with a grin. "See you tonight?"

I laugh and nod as she kisses me one last time and slips out the door. I flop back in bed and fold my arms behind my head, staring at the ceiling.

I breathe in deeply and close my eyes. I don't remember the last time I woke up with a beautiful woman in bed beside me and I didn't want to run away. This time it was her who wanted to run away.

I mull over her words. In one breath she's warning me against her and in the next, she's telling me she'll see me tonight. What does she mean, Mary Hanson can cause damage? What could that have to do with anything?

The town seems to have accepted me. Ever since the grand opening, the restaurant and bar have been full every night, and the rooms are starting to fill up with tourists for the start of the summer season.

Within a few months I should be able to put it back up for sale and turn a profit. Hell, maybe someone from the town will want to buy it up again.

I sigh. Jess is probably just paranoid because of what she's been through. Coming back here and facing all the people who shunned her must be difficult, and she can't see that it's different now.

I'll just have to show her it's different. Maybe I can convince her to go out with me in public, and she'll see that there's nothing to be afraid of. I only have a few more days with her, and I don't want to waste them hiding away in my room.

I stretch my arms overhead and sigh. I have another long day of work ahead of me, but it doesn't seem so bad when I think of Jess's goodbye kiss and her saying she would see me tonight. It's only a few short hours to fill before I can have her in my arms again.

28

JESS

"You didn't come home last night," Gram says as I walk in the door. I head to the coffee pot and pour a mug, avoiding her questioning stare.

"Late night with Sam. Did you know that her and Ronnie are engaged? You didn't tell me they were dating!"

Gram chuckles. "They've been loved up ever since he came back from Philadelphia. I thought you knew. I was sure Sam would have told you."

A pang passes through my heart. "I guess we haven't been talking so much lately," I say. Gram nods.

"How did Mr. McAllister get on with all the garden tools?"

"Great!" I say right away, maybe a bit too loud. "Great," I say again, burying my nose in my coffee mug.

"That's good. You make sure to thank him again from me for the hedges out front. I'm getting too old to garden now, it's nice to have someone make the place look nice."

"Sure, Gram, I'll say thanks, but I'm not sure when I'll see him again."

"Mm-hmm," Gram says, turning to the sink to wash a few dishes. "Okay, honey."

I look at the back of her head and can't help but smile. Does she know? How would she know!

Last night Sam and Ronnie could tell right away that there was something between us, but surely when Owen was here yesterday it wasn't that obvious? I shake my head and stand up.

"I'm going to go to the shop today, do you need me to bring you anything back?"

"Get some berries and a bit of beef," Gram says, glancing at the fridge. "I'll cook us a roast tonight."

"Sounds delicious," I say as I slip out of the kitchen. I make my way upstairs and flop down on my bed as soon as I'm in my room. I put a hand to my forehead and sigh.

For the first time since I left his room this morning, I feel like I can relax. I look around my childhood bedroom and shake my head. I never would have imagined that I'd be back here, having a secret love affair with the new owner of the Lex. I thought I'd come back and have some quiet evenings with Gram, see Sam and her mom, and maybe go into the Lex one night for a drink.

My phone buzzes and Rosie's name pops up.

Rosie: *So? Update?*

I grin.

Jess: I'm not coming back.

Rosie answers right away.

Rosie: *What? He's that good, huh?*

I laugh and turn onto my side, curling up in bed as I type my response.

Jess: *Better than good. Spent the night 🙄 trying to sneak around town so no one knows.*

The phone rings. "Hey Rosie," I say as I pick up.

"I got sick of texting. Tell. Me. Everything."

"Well, I went over last night and snuck in the back door of

the hotel to get up to his room." I pause as Rosie laughs. "It was like Mission Impossible to get up there."

"And then... you didn't sleep a wink because you were busy screwing each other's brains out?"

"Basically, yeah," I laugh.

"So what's the plan," she asks. "Are you going to keep talking to him? You weren't serious about staying there, were you?"

"No," I laugh. "I'll be back in New York in a couple days. I don't know what's going to happen. There's no future for me in this town, the only reason I'm here is to see my grandma. I can't imagine myself coming back here to be with a guy. It would be like moving backward."

"Well, you never know," Rosie says. A baby starts crying in the background and she sighs. "Whatever you do, just make sure you wear protection. You don't want to have the choice taken away from you."

"Don't worry," I laugh. "I am a baby-free zone and plan on being one for a long time."

"Yeah, well, so did I, and then I got pregnant," she laughs. "So take it from someone who knows and just be careful."

"All right. See you when I'm back."

"I expect a full debrief of ALL details."

"You'll get it," I laugh. "Whether you want to hear it all or not."

We hang up and I lean back in my bed, smiling. Her words ring in my ears and I think back to yesterday. We definitely wore a condom every time, I know we did. I take a deep breath and get up. After a shower and some food I'll be ready for another day and looking forward to another night with Owen.

29

OWEN

The next few days go by more quickly than I could imagine. Jess and I steal any moment we can together. Before I know it, it's the day before she leaves for New York. She walks into the hotel with a smile on her face and my chest tightens.

"Come on," she says. "I want to show you something."

We walk through the streets all the way to the edge of town in silence. Jess guides me to a small trail leading to some trees and then slips her hand into mine. Our fingers interlace and she moves a tiny bit closer to me. Even the feeling of her palm against mine makes my body buzz.

"Where are you taking me?" I ask. "Should I be worried?"

She laughs and then winks at me. "Very."

We walk a bit further before dipping between some tall pine trees. We follow what looks like an animal trail until the sound of rushing water gets louder. The trees open up on a small clearing at the edge of the river. We sit on a big rock and let our legs dangle over the edge, just above the flowing water.

Jess sighs before looking over at me and smiling. "Welcome to my special place," she says, turning back to the flowing water. "I used to come here when I was a kid. It was like my hideaway."

"It's beautiful here. This whole town is beautiful. I didn't think I'd like it so much." Jess's face darkens and she doesn't answer. We sit in silence until I finally speak again.

"Jess," I start. She turns to me and tilts her head to the side. "Why do you have such a negative view of this place? What happened? To me it seems like everyone is friendly and it's a really pleasant place to live."

She's silent for a long time. A bird sings in a tree behind us and the water flows under our feet. She leans against me and I wrap my arm around her shoulder. Sitting here, on this rock, she feels so slight in my arms. It feels like a strong gust of wind could knock her over.

"I was dating this guy in high school," she finally starts. "My first boyfriend. I was head over heels in love, you know how teenagers are." She pauses again and I feel a sigh rake through her body. "I got pregnant, and he ran."

She stops talking. I can feel her heart beating through her body and I squeeze her a bit tighter against me. Finally she takes a breath and keeps going.

"You know those rumors I told you about? The ones that drove me insane?"

I grunt in response and then clear my throat. "Yeah."

"Well, my boyfriend left me. I was pregnant and alone and terrified. These rumors started that I'd gotten an abortion in a back alley. I hadn't, obviously. I was still pregnant and everyone was whispering about me behind my back, staring at me as I walked past and not saying a word to me. One time I was spat on," she adds slowly. "And told that I was just like my mother."

Her body shudders and I look down to see her face

contorted in pain. I hold her a bit closer as my chest squeezes. My throat closes up and I don't know what to say. I want to take away her pain but I don't know how.

"I'm sorry, Jess," I finally whisper.

She shakes her head and sits up straighter. "I lost the baby. I was so confused. I was terrified, and I didn't know what to do, but a part of me wanted the baby." She looks over at me and smiles sadly, and then continues.

"They found out I had a miscarriage and not an abortion and apparently that was enough to forgive me and treat me like a human again. That's what really drove me crazy, it was going back to normal as if nothing happened. I couldn't even grieve the loss of my child, I had to pretend like nothing had ever happened. I started spiraling out of control. I took a bunch of pills one day to try to end it all."

"Jesus, Jess..." I breathe. My throat tightens some more and I turn to kiss the side of her head. She lifts her hands up and wipes her cheeks.

"You know that they say almost twenty percent of pregnancies end up in miscarriages?" She asks suddenly. I shake my head and she continues: "They don't tell you that in sex ed. They don't tell you that until you have one and it feels like your insides are being ripped out."

She chuckles bitterly and then turns to me. "Aren't you glad you came here with me today?" She says sarcastically. "I'm just a ball of sunshine."

I reach up and wipe a tear from her cheek. "Thank you for telling me," I say. She smiles.

"It was Gram who saved me," she says, and then laughs. "Saved me again, I mean. She helped me heal and got me to refocus on school. I'd have never gotten out of here if it wasn't for her."

"After all that, you got a full scholarship to Columbia? I mean, that seems like such a change, how...?"

She nods and then turns her head and smiles bitterly. "I was pretty desperate to get out," she laughs. "A bit of homework and extracurricular activities wasn't going to stop me."

I shake my head in disbelief. "I can't believe you've been through all that, and you still managed to get your life together again."

"I haven't told very many people the whole story," she says, swinging her eyes up to mine. "Even some of my best friends don't know."

"Why did you tell me?"

She's quiet for a long moment as she stares at me and chews her lips. Finally she shrugs. "I don't know. I wanted you to know."

She turns back to the river and nuzzles her head into my shoulder. I put my arm around her and pull her closer. My lips nuzzle into her hair and I kiss the top of her head. She moans gently and leans into me a little bit more.

The words catch in my throat. I want to tell her my story. I want to tell her about working for my father and being accused of fraud. Everything she went through, people whispering about her and talking behind her back—I went through it all, and for me it was plastered on all the newspapers. I know how she felt, because I've been through it too. I'm surprised she hasn't recognized me.

The charges against me were dropped, and everything was supposed to go back to normal. That's why I left New York, and that's why she left here. I've never met anyone who understands that, let alone someone who's lived it. I want to tell her everything, but how could I betray my father like that? He's still in the middle of the trial, and I just want to get away from it all.

I lean my head against hers and follow her gaze toward the water. We sit in silence, side by side, hearts beating together as we watch the river flow on and on and on.

30

JESS

It feels good to tell him everything. I don't even know why I told him, but it feels good to sit here quietly and know that he knows my past. Well, not everything. I didn't tell him that it was Mary Hanson who started the rumors, and it was her who spat on me. I don't need to tell him that. I don't want to name names and make him look at people differently or put negative ideas into his head. I'd rather just leave it all behind.

I am leaving it all behind all over again. I leave tomorrow. Usually I'm relieved to get out of this town, but now it feels bittersweet. I lean my head into Owen's shoulder and sigh. Why did it have to be here that I met him? In this town! Surrounded by all these people that have been the source of all my pain!

As if he can sense my unease, Owen pulls me closer and lifts his head. He brings his hand up to my chin and turns my face up to his.

When he kisses me, it doesn't feel like the burning passion that we've had all week. It doesn't feel like we're about to tear each other's clothes off any second. Instead, he kisses me gently, sweetly. It sends a warmth through my body, spreading from my heart to every extremity. Suddenly my heart starts beating harder inside my hollow chest and he strokes the side of my face. He keeps kissing me and kissing me until I'm not sure if I'm hearing the river or my own heartbeat in my ears.

Finally, our lips come apart and we stare into each other's eyes. His dark brown eyes are shining as he tucks my hair behind my ear.

"You're incredible, Jess, you know that?" He says softly. My heart beats against my ribcage and I try to swallow. "I'm glad I met you."

The words pass through me and it feels like there's true meaning behind them. He strokes my face again and smiles gently.

"I'm glad I met you too," I croak. My voice is gone and it's hard for me to swallow. Owen pulls me closer but instead of kissing me again, he wraps his arms around me tightly and holds me against him. I shudder and melt into his chest as all the tension in my bones dissolves with his touch. He strokes my hair and holds me tight until my whole body relaxes.

I've never felt so safe or so at home as I do in this instant. I tilt my head up to meet his eye again and he moves his mouth to meet mine. I trail my fingers along his jaw, feeling the rough stubble as our lips crush together. He holds me closer than I've ever been held, and I feel more connected to him right now than I have to anyone else.

I don't think I knew the meaning of *making love* until today. I don't think I even imagined it was any different from regular sex.

Now I know.

It's more than different—it's a completely new experience. Every touch, however gentle, feels electric. Every look feels like it's a physical touch, and every noise sends vibrations through my body. It's less like sex and more like a dance that our bodies instinctively know. Our limbs are intertwined and our lips find each other so that every kiss is more tender than the last.

We make love by the river, in the one place in this town that I've always felt safe. We make love with the blue skies overhead and the birds singing in the trees, and the cleansing water rushing past beside us. We make love and nothing in this world matters more than the man in my arms and the beating of my heart in my chest.

When it's over, we lie in the grassy clearing, staring at the clouds as they change shape and take a deep breath and sigh. Owen squeezes his arm around me and I smile. We don't speak, because we don't have to. It's like our bodies have a language of their own, and every touch tells a million stories.

The clouds puff and shift in the sky and the birds keep singing. The water keeps flowing and the two of us lie there in silence, perfectly content. This must be what happiness feels like.

31

OWEN

We walk back, hand in hand. We turn toward her grandmother's house and my chest tightens. I won't see her tonight, or the next night, or for countless nights after that until she's back for Sam's wedding.

"I might be able to come to New York to see you. Two months seems like a long time," I say as we walk under the shady trees.

Jess turns to me and smiles. "That would be nice."

My heart does a backflip and I smile. She wants to see me again! We step out of the forest onto the edge of town and Jess squeezes my hand. I glance at her and hold our interlocked fingers up.

"You're holding my hand in public," I say slowly. "Aren't you worried about someone seeing us?"

"Fuck 'em," she says with a grin. We both start laughing and I squeeze her hand a bit tighter.

"Yeah," I say softly. "Fuck 'em."

I don't understand what's going on inside me. I know I'm sad that she's leaving, but it's way more intense than I'd expect. I only just met her! I wish we'd had more time to get to know each other. She's just opened up to me, and given me a glimpse of who she really is. We're only just exploring each other's bodies and still making each other laugh all the time.

I'm on a high, and she's leaving.

"You sure you don't want to stay just a couple days longer?" I ask, glancing over at her. She smiles and looks up at me. There's something in her eyes that I can't place.

"Tempting," she says. I can't tell if she's being sarcastic or not so I say nothing. She smiles again, a bit more sadly this time. "I have to go back to work. I wish I could stay. Actually, I wish you could come with me," she laughs. "That would be the best option."

I would if I could.

"Can I come visit you?" My voice sounds insecure and thin, even to my ears. I steal a glance at Jess's face and she squeezes my hand. I can hardly hear her when she speaks.

"I'd like that," she says. She turns her head and smiles at me again. This time her smile travels all the way up to her eyes. Her cheeks start to flush and her eyes look almost misty. "I'd like that a lot."

"Done," I say. She smiles again and turns her head forward. We're rounding the last corner to her grandmother's house. Both of us are walking impossibly slowly. I want to savor every single second that we have together, and the inevitable goodbye is looming closer with every step.

Jess holds my hand a bit tighter as we get closer to the house. It feels like there's a hand gripping my throat, stopping me from swallowing. My vision starts to blur and I quickly blink to clear my eyes.

Finally, we get to those familiar flagstones and walk up to her grandmother's porch. Jess steps onto the first step and I pause. She turns to me and puts her hands on my shoulders. With her standing on the step, we're exactly eye to eye. She smiles at me and runs her fingers along my shoulders and back to the nape of my neck. I feel her interlace her fingers behind me as I slide my hands onto her waist.

"This was a surprisingly pleasant visit," she says. "I never thought I'd meet someone like you here."

"And I never thought I'd meet someone like you… anywhere, really. Especially not here."

Jess laughs and my heart starts to crack. I love the way the laughter makes her shoulders bounce up and down and how she tilts her head back and laughs as if no one is watching. I chuckle with her. I can't help it.

"You're so different from other girls," I say.

Jess shakes her head and smiles at me. "No I'm not," she replies. "I'm not different or special or anything. You and I just happened to click. We get along, and we found each other in this crazy town. That's what's special, not me or you."

"Are you saying I'm not special," I answer as the corner of my lip starts to lift upward.

She grins. "Not even a little bit."

Before I can answer, her lips are on mine and I get to taste her kiss for the last time today. I pull her waist toward me and crush my lips against hers. She tangles her fingers into my hair and presses her body against me. My cock throbs in my pants and I wish she wasn't leaving, not yet.

She pulls away from me and laughs. "Well if no one saw us holding hands, they definitely saw that."

"Fuck 'em," I say with a smile. "Isn't that what you said?"

"I did say that," she concedes. "And I stand by it."

She leans forward and lays one last soft kiss on my lips before pulling away. Her hands drag off my shoulders and fall to her sides as she turns slowly and walks up the steps. She opens the door and glances at me one last time. She smiles softly.

"See you soon," she says.

I nod. "See you soon."

32

JESS

"So are you going to keep seeing him?" Harper asks as she leans across the table. We're at our favorite brunch spot and I'm staring at my plate full of Belgian waffles, piled high with fresh fruit and whipped cream. Call it comfort eating after a difficult goodbye.

"Yeah, he said he'd come to New York in a couple weeks," I answer as I cut a sliver of the waffle and poke my fork into it.

"No fucking way," Rosie says, shaking her head and smirking. "You, the queen of the single life, are smitten."

I lean back. "Smitten! What?"

Rosie raises an eyebrow and laughs. "I know that look. It's the same look I had on my face when I met Lucas. It's the look that says, 'I'm completely fucked. I'm not getting out of this one in one piece'"

I laugh. "Maybe I am smitten. I have no hope."

"Not a chance," Rosie answers with a laugh. "You're going to end up heartbroken or married. There's no in between."

I groan. "Neither of those sound particularly appealing. Can't we just settle for dating?"

"There's no in between," Harper says. She shakes her

head and I go back to my waffle. The two of them laugh and I roll my eyes before grinning at them.

"So come on," Rosie says. "Show us a picture."

"If you insist," I laugh as I lunge for my phone. "Let me find a good one."

Rosie and Harper make the appropriate oohs and ahhs when I flick through his social media profile, and both lean back with an approving nod.

Harper takes a bite of her food and chews thoughtfully. "Owen McAllister. Why does that name ring a bell?"

I shrug. "No idea. He used to live in New York, maybe you met him?"

Harper shakes her head and shrugs. "Maybe. It just sounds familiar."

"Show us another picture, maybe we'll be able to figure it out," Rosie says as she wiggles her eyebrows.

We all laugh and I pick up my phone. "If you insist. I don't mind looking at photos of him all day long."

"Like I said: smitten." Rosie looks at me with a smirk on her face and I laugh.

When we leave the restaurant, Rosie gives me a big hug.

"Make sure you introduce him to us when he comes to town," she says. "I'm happy for you. You deserve to be happy."

I can't help but smile. "Thanks Rosie. I will. And even if you don't meet him, I'll tell you everything so it'll feel like you've already met him."

"I'm sure you will," she laughs.

We part ways and I make my way back to my apartment. When the door closes behind me, my phone buzzes. It's Harper.

Harper: *I googled him. I knew I recognized the name!*

Attached to the text is an article. I read the headline and frown.

BILLIONAIRE'S SON ACCUSED OF FRAUD, AVOIDS JAIL TIME

I click the link as my heart drops. I scan the article but I already know what it says. I remember this story from months ago. The city's biggest real estate investment mogul, Richard McAllister, was accused of fraud. His whole company was investigated and he's still going through the trial. They'd been turning run-down apartment blocks and businesses for profit, but siphoning money and grossly misreporting costs. They used shoddy building techniques to make a quick buck, leaving the new owners to pick up the pieces. They were scammers.

His entire company was investigated, including his second-in-command and eldest son: Owen McAllister.

My hands are shaking. It can't be him! I read the article again and again and click a related link at the bottom. Within a fraction of a second, Owen's face appears in front of the courthouse. He's lifting his hand to cover his face from the cameras but I can still see it. It's him.

The man that I've opened up to, the man that I trusted with my story and my secrets, the man that I just spent the happiest week I've ever had is a scumbag.

I sit down on the couch as my phone buzzes again and again. It's Harper. She's texting and calling but I don't have the heart or the energy to pick up right now. I just keep looking at the photo of Owen in front of the courthouse.

He's a criminal. He's a fraud.

And now, he's in my hometown doing the same. Fucking. Thing. He's scamming the people I grew up with. He scammed me! No wonder I'm smitten, he's nothing more than a con man.

The heat starts flowing through my veins as my anger starts to boil. My hands are shaking and I throw my phone across the room. I grab a pillow beside me on the sofa and press it to my face, screaming as loud as I possibly can. The pillow muffles the sound and I take it away from my face, panting.

I take a deep breath and bring the pillow back up, screaming into it with all my lungs before throwing it away. It lands on the coffee table and knocks off a couple magazines. They fall in a heap on the floor and all I can do is sit there and stare at them. My chest is heaving up and down and all I can do is feel the anger as it boils through me.

My emotion is tinged with something else—embarrassment, maybe? Embarrassed that I fell for it, that I fell for his charm and his smiles and his words. Embarrassed that I didn't question why he'd chosen that small town, that hotel. Embarrassed that I didn't press him to know why he left.

Embarrassed that I didn't google his fucking name even once.

Obviously, the gossip had some truth to it. He was running away from something. It wasn't a grisly murder or a divorce, but it was still a crime.

33

OWEN

I'M WHISTLING as I pat the dark earth around the new plants that line the front of the Lexington Hotel. I didn't even know I was able to whistle, but it just started coming out of me. I stand up and lean against my shovel to admire my handiwork.

I'm proud of this place. It used to be a run-down hotel and now it's the town's crown jewel. It feels good to do something like this, to do something real. It might not have the profit margin that my father expected when I worked for him, but at least it's good, honest hard work.

"Looking good," comes an overly sweet drawl from behind me. Mary's standing with her hip cocked to one side, looking me up and down. "The flowers, I mean," she adds with a smirk.

"Thanks. How's your husband?" I ask. She looks taken aback but recovers quickly.

"Fiancé," she corrects. "He's good." She sashays past me and goes up the steps. Instead of heading inside, she leans against the railing on the balcony, pushing her chest toward me. I try not to roll my eyes. I'm glad I'm not her fiancé.

"So," she starts. "You and Jessica Lee, huh?"

"What do you mean," I ask, sticking the shovel into the ground and turning over the earth I'd just patted down.

"You two are an item now, I guess, aren't you?"

"What business is that of yours?" I ask, finally glancing up at her again. That smirk is still playing on her lips and she shrugs innocently.

"Oh, it isn't any of my business. I just thought with you being new in town you might not have the full story."

I try to ignore her but I can't help myself. The curiosity needles at me until I have to ask. "What's the full story?"

Mary waves a hand and turns around to lean against the railing. She swings a leg over so she's straddling it, looking down at me as her hair swings down on one side of her face. She licks her lips slowly and grins.

"Jessica Lee got into all sorts of trouble. She's not the kind of girl that a respectable business owner such as yourself should be hanging around with."

"Everyone has their past," I answer, driving the shovel back into the ground with a little too much force.

"Well, everyone has a past, but not everyone screws their way into a full scholarship at a top college."

I can't help it. My jaw drops open and I look up at Mary. She looks almost triumphant as she nods at me.

"Honest to goodness truth. I don't blame you for falling for her charms. She's gotten lots of practice. Even tried it with my fiancé. Before he was my fiancé, obviously."

I shake my head and pick up the shovel. "I don't want to hear this. Isn't your shift already started?"

Mary shrugs and I feel her eyes on me as I walk around the corner toward the back of the hotel. I'm panting. My chest is heaving up and down as I make the short walk to the back.

As soon as I'm in the shed, I put the shovel down and lean against the wall. I rub my face in my hands and sigh.

Surely, she was lying? She couldn't be telling the truth? Jess told me that people here like to talk, that they tortured her after she got pregnant. She said they treated her like an outsider until she lost the baby. That's who Mary is.

It just doesn't sound like something Jess would do. It doesn't fit with the story she told me by the river. But then again... how *did* she get into a top college after all that? It sounds almost plausible, if I didn't know Jess.

I *don't* know Jess. I don't know her at all! I met her two weeks ago! Who am I to tell which story is the truth! She could be playing me, or just using me for sex while she's here. She's only called me once since she got back to New York, which was three days ago already!

My breath is heaving now, and my mind is reeling. I don't know what to think. I don't know what the truth is. I don't know who Jess is, or why the thought of her sleeping around with anyone to get what she wants bothers me as much as it does. I don't even know if it's true!

I take a deep breath and shake my head. I need to find out the truth. If I'm going to go all the way to New York to visit her, I want to know that she's the type of girl that's worth trusting.

34

JESS

"Jess, you're like, the social media stalker queen. How did you not realize who he was?" Rosie is shaking her head in disbelief. "His face was all over the news for months!"

"I'm the social media stalker queen, I don't watch the news! Two different things," I protest. "Plus, I showed you pictures and you didn't recognize him either."

"True," she concedes. She purses her lips and keeps bouncing her little boy on her knee.

"Here, hold him, I need to go pee."

Before I know what's happening, Rosie thrusts her baby into my arms and stands up, brushing off her thighs.

"Wait! Ah," I say, juggling the little human in my hands. Jack flops back and forth, arms flailing around and giggles as I sit him upright. My heart is thumping and I stare at Rosie, wide-eyed.

"Relax. Just don't drop him," Rosie says with a laugh.

"Oh, yeah, okay, sure. Just don't drop him," I shoot back at her as she laughs and walks away. The door to the bathroom closes and I can almost hear Rosie sighing with relief. This baby has been tied to her hip ever since he was born, I can only imagine the relief of being alone for even a couple minutes.

I turn Jack to look at me, holding his chubby little body between my hands. He looks at me curiously, chewing on his fingers. His bright blue eyes are staring at me intently.

"What are you looking at," I say under my breath. "Don't tell me you're judging me as well. I swear I didn't know who he was!"

Jack giggles and takes his hand out of his mouth, flinging spit toward me as he points his finger at me. He falls forward, laughing the whole way as he collides with my stomach. I lean back on the sofa and hold him against me. He kneads my stomach and chest as he giggles, and finally head-butts me in the boob.

I laugh. "Already all about the boobs, are you, Jack? Must be instinct."

Something stirs inside me as Jack giggles again and reaches up to my face. His tiny fingers brush my mouth and I kiss them gently. I hold his little arm in my hand and give his fingers another kiss.

"He likes you," Rosie says as she walks back in. I jump and start moving toward her. "No, no, you hold him. It's nice to have a break."

I sit back and Jack settles back into me.

"I can't believe how soft his skin is," I breathe.

"I know. All these creams and serums and every day I'm reminded of what my skin used to be," Rosie says wistfully. "It's so not fair."

I laugh and shake my head. The baby shuffles against me and I feel that same tightening of my core. I stroke his back, up and down his spine and he settles down against me. Within seconds, he's asleep. Rosie whistles.

"We should keep you around more often," she says with a laugh. "I never get him to bed that easily."

"I'm afraid to move," I say in a whisper.

Rosie laughs. "Don't be. You're really good with him, you know. You sure you don't want kids?"

"Definitely not," I say, but there's no force behind my words. I look at Jack and brush his thin hair off his forehead. Suddenly my 'definitely not' feels more like a 'maybe'.

What if I had a baby of my own? I glance up at Rosie and catch her looking at Jack as if he's the most precious thing in the world. He is, to her. Her eyes flick up to mine and she smiles.

"Best thing that ever happened to me," she says. "But don't you go and get pregnant like I did. I got lucky."

"You definitely got lucky. Lucas was head over heels in love with you from the first day. And here I am, perma-single. And if I'm not perma-single, I'm pursuing literal *criminals*."

Rosie laughs. "He was acquitted, wasn't he? Or the charges were dropped?"

"Yeah, but then he goes and buys a run-down hotel in my hometown to try to flip it? Come on."

Rosie sighs and shakes her head. "It's such a shame. I haven't seen that spark in your eye in I don't know how long... maybe ever. The way you were talking about him reminded me of Harper and Zach, way back in the day."

Jack starts snoring gently and wriggles as he sleeps. I chuckle and stroke his back. My hand covers almost his entire body and I lean down to kiss the top of his head.

Do I want this?

I shake my head and sigh. Even if I do want this, it's not like it's an option right now.

"Just going to have to start back at square one. New York has what, like eight and a half million people? So at least four million dudes? Surely ONE of them is okay? Is that too much to ask?"

Rosie smiles sadly. "You'll find someone. Don't worry, Jess."

"I'm not worried. I've always been happy being single! Fuck, I mean I *am* happy being single," I say. I look down at Jack. "Sorry for swearing." I look back at Rosie who chuckles as I keep talking. "I think being with Owen back in my hometown just made me see a different side of relationships. Like, I could see the good side of it. And you and Harper and my friend Sam are all getting married and having babies and what am I doing?"

I sigh and Rosie comes to sit next to me. She puts her arm around me and leans her head against mine.

"Chin up, Jess. You should ask him about it. Don't just cut him out. Learn from my mistakes with Lucas. Just talk to him and see what he says. If the love is there, it's worth fighting for."

"Love," I say with a snort. "Is that what this is? Doesn't feel like love."

Rosie just grins at me and shrugs. Just then, Jack wakes up and starts wailing. Rosie makes motherly noises and grabs him, bouncing him over her shoulder. I stand up.

"I'll leave you to it. Thanks Rosie."

"Anytime," she says with a smile. I lean over and kiss her on the cheek, and then kiss Jack as he screams his head off. I wave goodbye as she turns to Jack's bedroom. I can still hear the sound of his crying as I close the door behind me and head out toward the street.

No, I don't want that. It looks exhausting and tireless. I definitely don't want that.

But as I walk away, I can still smell Jack's fresh baby scent on me, and I can still feel his impossibly soft skin under my fingers. I think of the way Rosie was looking at him with complete adoration in her eyes, and I can't help but wonder what it would feel like to have a kid of my own.

35

OWEN

AFTER THREE DAYS of complete silence, the phone finally rings and Jess's name appears on the screen. I sit down in my office chair and pick it up, hovering my finger over the 'Ignore' button. With a deep breath, I decide to not be petty and click the green button to answer.

"Hey," I say into the phone.

"Hey," comes her voice. I can't help it, even hearing that one word, even hearing the hesitation in the way she's speaking doesn't stop my heart from beating a little bit harder. I take a deep breath and wait for her to speak.

"So, how are you?" Her voice sounds so forced. I frown and let out a sigh.

"I'm fine. What's going on, Jess? I thought... I don't know what I thought. I thought you wanted to keep seeing me, but now I've hardly heard from you at all since you left."

"I did! I do! I mean,..." Her voice trails off and I wait. She takes a deep breath and lets it out. It blows into the phone and I wait for her to speak. "I googled you," she finally says.

My heart drops like a stone. Her words sound so final. I've

heard it before. Ever since the trial, I've been thrown out of restaurants, had backs turned on me, been shut out of the social circles where I used to thrive. And for what? For my father's mistakes?

"Right," I respond. "The trial."

"Yes, the trial," she spits. "When I asked you why you left New York, you didn't think being accused of millions of dollars' worth of fraud qualified?"

"Why would I need to tell you anything?" I almost shout.

She gasps. "I opened up to you, Owen. I told you things that I've never told anyone before. And now you're asking why you would tell me anything? How can you sit there and tell me that you're upset I haven't called you in one breath, and in the next you justify not telling me that you were convicted of a FELONY!"

"I didn't do it! I didn't do any of it and it's been following me around for months. I wanted you to get to know me for me and not run off and look up my name and everything that people said about me and my family."

"Right."

"The charges were dropped."

"Did you know it was happening?"

"No! I swear," I say. I put a hand to my forehead. "I swear. I didn't know until the trial."

"So your father was syphoning millions of dollars into his own pockets and you had no idea?" I can hear the incredulity in her voice.

"No, I swear, Jess. I didn't know. If I had known I would have done something."

I can hear her breathing on the other end of the phone but she says nothing. The anger starts to grow inside me as she remains silent. How dare she call me and accuse me of these things! Instead of talking to me like an adult and asking me for my side, she just reads tabloids and accuses me of the same things all over again!

"You're no angel yourself," I find myself snarling into the phone. "I've heard about how you got into Columbia."

"Columbia?" She sounds genuinely confused, but my anger doesn't let me acknowledge it. I keep going.

"Yeah. Columbia. You made me believe you worked and turned yourself around and got in on your own merit. What a crock of shit that was. Yeah, I heard the stories."

"A crock of shit?"

"And sneaking around with Mary Hanson's fiancé, Christ, Jess, it's like you have no shame at all. You made me believe that you wanted to keep us quiet to protect me, but you were just protecting your own reputation in this town. Well, let me fill you in: you have no reputation here. It's not salvageable."

I can feel the anger radiating through the phone. "Mary Hanson," Jess says in a complete deadpan voice. "You're telling me that you believe Mary Hanson over me?"

"Yes, I do, actually," I spit out.

"Owen, I don't even know who Mary Hanson's fiancé *is*. The guy I supposedly messed around with behind her back. I got a scholarship to Columbia because I had the best SAT scores in the state. Oh, and fuck you."

The phone clicks off and I stare at the blank screen. My heart is pounding and her words ring in my ears.

"Fuck," I say under my breath. "Fuck, fuck, fuck!"

My hands are shaking as I try to dial her number again. It rings.

"Come on, come on, answer, Jess, please," I whisper to myself. Halfway through the next ring, it goes straight to voicemail and I hang up, throwing my phone down and putting my head in my hands.

Fuck.

I lean back in my chair and stare at the ceiling, trying to understand what just happened. I mean, I *know* what just happened—we got into a massive fight. She came out swinging about the trial and I lashed out.

This is the first woman that I actually started to care about, the first woman who held my interest for more than a few hours, the most intelligent and beautiful woman I've ever met, and what did I do? I accused her of sleeping around, of sleeping her way into college and I let her open up to me without telling her anything about myself.

I take a deep breath and stare at my black phone. I sigh. I don't know how to fix this. I don't even know if I can fix this.

There's a knock on the door and Joe pokes his head in.

"Hey, boss. Just letting you know… you okay?" He frowns as he looks at me.

"Yeah, I'm fine. What is it?"

"Nothing, I'll sort it out. You sure you're okay?"

"I'm fine, Joe." He nods and turns to leave before I call him back. "Joe, how much do you trust Mary?"

His eyebrow moves ever so slightly upward. It's an almost imperceptible movement, and his voice is completely flat. "Trust her with what?"

"If she told you something about someone."

Joe's shoulders relax and he lets out a snort. "I'd trust her about as far as I can throw her. No, I'd trust her as far as she can throw me," he says with a laugh, running his hands over his belly.

I chuckle bitterly and nod. "Right. Thanks, Joe."

He grunts and closes the door as he leaves.

I can't believe I said those things to Jess, that I accused her of all the things that Mary told me. I knew they weren't true and I still threw them in her face. Of course they weren't true! I rub my hands over my face and sigh again.

How the hell will she ever forgive me for saying those things to her? How the fuck am I going to get her to trust me after I hid my past from her?

36

JESS

BLOCK. Delete. Ignore.

That's the advice I would give any of my girlfriends if they were in my situation right now. But as my finger hovers over the word 'block', my whole body is shaking and the tears are streaming down my face.

I thought he was different. I thought he cared about me, but at the first sign of conflict he did exactly what everyone in that fucking town did to me when I was sixteen—shut me out and accuse me of being a whore.

Well, fuck him.

My finger drops down and his number is blocked. Before I can change my mind, I delete his number and flick to every app where we've connected. Social media, email, phone. Block, delete, ignore.

He's shown his true colors, and all it took was a week apart.

What was I thinking? Of course this would end in disaster. Who am I to think I'll meet my prince charming and live happily ever after? I was fucking dreaming. Even if he wasn't a criminal before moving to that town, living there would poison anyone's mind.

I put my phone down and head to the bathroom. In seconds I've stripped my clothes off and I'm standing under a burning jet of hot water. I let it wash over me for a few seconds, standing completely still, until the reality of what's just happened hits me.

The sobs start in my stomach, and my whole body shakes. They come up and scrape the back of my throat before erupting out of me, making me double over as I cry under the running water.

I cry and cry and cry until it hurts. Everything hurts. My skin is raw from the hot water, my throat is raw from the sobs. My eyes are puffy and my whole body feels swollen. Finally, my sobs quiet down and I wash myself, moving slowly and gently until my pain turns to numbness and my body is clean.

The bathroom is completely steamed up, and I'm glad I can't see in the mirror. I don't want to see what I look like right now. I wrap a towel around myself and shuffle to the bedroom, climbing under the covers and huddling into a ball.

My hair will be sticking up in a thousand directions if I sleep on it like this, and my eyes will be swollen shut when I wake up, but none of that matters.

My pain turned to numbness and now all I feel is a crushing tiredness. My bones feel tired, and every movement is difficult. I lay in bed in my towel and wrap the blankets around me, tuck my chin into my chest and hug myself until I fall asleep.

WHEN I WAKE UP, everything aches. I move slowly, checking the time on my phone before heading to the bathroom. It's 7 p.m., which means I slept for three hours. The steam on the bathroom mirror has long since cleared and I stare at myself in silence.

I wasn't wrong.

My eyes are so swollen I hardly recognize myself. My hair is almost dry, with a flat patch on one side of my head and frizzy curls on the other. I sigh, turning the tap on to cold water to wash my face.

I head to the kitchen and pour myself a glass of wine from a half-empty bottle before shaking my head and chuckling bitterly. I am the typical depressed woman, drinking wine alone in her apartment after crying in the shower and then napping. I'm still wearing my towel.

I knew the guy for a week, for fuck's sake. It's not like we were married. It's not like he cheated on me, or abused me. It just didn't work out. I had my cry and now I should just move on.

Still, the thought of Owen makes my chest ache. I bring my glass of wine to my lips and close my eyes as I swallow. I can almost feel the touch of his arms around my body, and the taste of his lips against mine. I can almost feel the way he would brush his lips against my neck or the way he'd pull me closer and sink his fingers into my body.

Almost, but not quite.

I open my eyes again and stand up a bit straighter before finishing my wine in one gulp.

This isn't me.

I knew the guy for a week, and now it's over. He said all the horrible things that everyone in my home town used to say to me, and that's unforgivable. I moved away for a reason, and I'm not going to let the promise of good sex and some cuddles drag me back there.

The bottle of wine is almost empty, so I dump the rest of it into my glass. I pull some sweatpants on and wrap a comfy sweatshirt around my body, and then curl up on the sofa with my wine. I put on a movie and settle in to my couch.

It's hard to get comfortable. The pillows are either too lumpy or too hard or too small. I remember lying in the grass with Owen after we made love and my chest squeezes, but I shake my head to forget it.

I've spent many nights alone in this apartment with a glass of wine and a movie, and I've been perfectly happy. It's no different now.

As I struggle to get comfortable, I admit to myself that it is different. It's completely different. I may have spent lots of time alone, but this is the first time I feel truly lonely. There's no one to wrap their arms around me, or to stroke my hair, or to kiss me on the temple. There's no strong chest to lean against, no other heartbeat to listen to as I drift off to sleep.

There's just me, my wine, and my movie, and it's starting to feel like it's not enough anymore.

37

OWEN

SHE'S BLOCKED ME EVERYWHERE. That's as clear a message as I need. She's moving on. Whatever we had, however great that week together was, it's over. She's gone, and I'm here, and that's that. It was a fling, and we both need to move on.

Even if I wanted to reach out and talk to her, to explain my past, to apologize for saying those things to her, I can't. I don't know where she lives or where she works, and even if I did, what would I do—show up at her work and beg her to talk to me? If that's not creepy then I don't know what is. This isn't some Hollywood rom-com.

The weeks go by and the hotel gets busier and busier as we move into summer. The first couple weeks, every time I lie in bed, I see her face beside me. Every time I grab something from the shed, I see her standing there in her blue dress. Every time I hear the birds singing, I remember the day by the river when I started falling for her.

How can one week feel so long? I feel like I've known her my whole life, but she just appeared and then disappeared just as quickly.

Business is booming, and the townspeople seem to have accepted me, or at the very least they tolerate me. The bar is busy every weekend, and the hotel gets more and more people every week. Everything is going well. Profits are through the roof. It's more successful than I could have imagined, but it still feels stale.

This isn't my town. This isn't my home. Even if it was, I can't seem to shake Jess from my mind. Everywhere I turn, something reminds me of her. I can hardly look her grandmother in the eye. The other day she gave me advice for the front flowerbed, and I couldn't focus on what she was saying because I was too busy thinking of Jess.

The only way I'll be able to forget about her is to sell this place and move on, but every time I think about putting it up on the market, something holds me back. Maybe I'm starting to feel at home here, or maybe I'm just waiting for Jess to come back.

ONE TUESDAY MORNING, the sun is shining and I'm sweeping the wide front porch of the hotel.

"Owen!" I hear as someone walks down the sidewalk toward me. It's Sam, Jess's childhood friend. She's got long brown hair, stick-straight, tied into a low ponytail. She walks up and gives me a warm smile.

"Hi, Sam, beautiful day, isn't it?"

"Gorgeous," she says, staring off into the sky. She turns back to me. "Hey, Owen, I was wondering if I could ask you something."

I stand up a bit straighter and nod, waiting for her to speak.

"Well, I'm getting married in four weeks, and I was planning on having the reception at my mother's house."

I nod, and she continues.

"Well," she says, turning her palms up to, "Ronnie's family have decided to invite themselves, and you know I can't say no. We don't have room for all those people."

"Right," I answer slowly.

"Now I know it's the fourth of July, and you'll be busy here, but I was wondering if there was any way we could use the Lex as our reception hall? It doesn't have to be anything fancy. We'll pay you, of course."

I smile and nod. "Of course, Sam. I didn't have anything big planned. I hadn't booked a band yet or anything. The whole town was going to be at your wedding anyways, so this might work out for the both of us," I laugh.

Sam chuckles. "I figured that," she says with a grin. "Well, that's a relief. I'll come by tomorrow with the details and we can sort it out, if that works for you?"

"Sure thing," I reply. She smiles at me and walks on toward the corner store. I watch her go inside and hear the little bell jingle before I let out a sigh.

That means Jess will be here. She's the maid of honor, of course she'll be here. I wonder if there's any way I can avoid the wedding? Maybe I can put Joe in charge of it, and I can take the day off and go do a trip somewhere.

I glance back at the bar and take a deep breath.

Don't be ridiculous.

I'm an adult. Jess and I had a fling, it lasted a week. Her best friend is getting married and I happen to own the hotel in town. This doesn't have to be a big deal. It's not a big deal! She'll probably be so busy with Sam that I won't even see her at all.

This is fine. This is completely fine.

I brush the broom back and forth a little bit harder. It scrapes against the old wood porch, back and forth, until the sweat starts dripping off my face. I stand up and take a deep breath, wiping my forearm across my forehead.

This is fine. This is completely, totally fine.

38

JESS

I DON'T THINK about Owen so much anymore. The first couple weeks were hard but now, after almost two months, I'm pretty much back to normal. It was a fling, nothing more. It burned hot and then fizzled and then I moved on.

That's what I tell myself, anyways.

I tuck my hair behind my ear before walking into our regular brunch restaurant. I can see Harper and Rosie through the window, looking at the menus even though I know we're all going to order the same thing as usual. Waffles for me, eggs benedict for Harper, and a big stack of pancakes for Rosie. Even though they're married with kids, at least some things don't change.

"Jess!" Rosie calls out with a smile. "You ready for the big day?"

I laugh. "Always a bridesmaid. Or whatever."

"So you leave tomorrow?" Harper asks, closing the menu and taking a sip of coffee.

"Yep, tomorrow."

"And have you spoken to Owen?"

I shake my head. "Not since he accused me of sleeping around."

Rosie and Harper nod in unison. I open the menu up and scan the food just to avoid their stare.

"So, are you nervous?" Rosie asks slowly. I glance up and see her looking at me expectantly.

I shrug. "About the wedding? No."

"No," Rosie chuckles. "About seeing Owen."

"Right. Umm. No, not nervous."

They both laugh as I shake my head vigorously. "Not nervous at all?" Harper asks.

"Okay, fine," I answer with a smile, closing my menu up. "Maybe a little nervous. I can't help it! The last time we spoke I hung up on him and deleted his number.

"Didn't you say that the reception was moved to the hotel?" Rosie asks with a frown

"Yeah." I remember how my stomach dropped when Sam called to tell me that. "Look, for all I know he's sold the hotel and moved away. I don't even know if I'll see him."

"What are you going to do if you do see him?" Harper asks. "Are you going to sleep with him?"

"What is this, the Spanish Inquisition?" I say with a laugh. "I thought I was getting breakfast here, not an interrogation."

They both laugh and sit back. "Fine," says Rosie. "Sorry."

Our usual waitress, Meg, walks up to our table with a smile. "Morning, ladies. The usual?

"Yep!" The three of us answer. The waitress looks at me and tilts her head to the side.

"Jess. You look absolutely glowing this morning! Do you have a new skincare routine? Where can I get what you have!"

"Aw, thanks Meg," I smile. "Nope, nothing new. I have

been trying to drink more water, maybe that's made a difference."

"I'll have to try that," she answers with a wink.

Harper looks at me curiously. "You do look like you're glowing. Maybe you're looking forward to rekindling your romance with the felon."

Rosie laughs. "Did you even delete his number? What are you hiding from us?"

"You guys are relentless," I say with a laugh. "Why can't it just be that I'm drinking more water? Isn't that a great reason for my skin to look good? I got a new moisturizer as well."

"Mm," Rosie says as she narrows her eyes. "But there's skin looking good and then there's a glow. That comes from within, and it's not because of water or cream."

"Well, whatever," I say. "How are the kids?"

My two friends lean back and start talking about their children. Usually I'd zone out at this point, but today I'm interested. I like hearing about what they said, or how they're walking, or the funny things they're doing.

Before I know it, steaming plates of food are being dropped off at the table. My usual stack of waffles comes piled high with strawberries and whipped cream. They look exactly the same as every other time I've ordered them, but this time when the sweet, doughy odor hits my nose, it makes my stomach churn.

I take one look at the waffles and put my hand to my mouth.

"Excuse me," I say without looking at the girls.

In a moment I'm sprinting through the restaurant toward the bathrooms. I smash through the door and thankfully find the first stall free. My stomach heaves and I throw up. The bile burns my throat as it comes up my esophagus. Soon I'm panting, leaning against the toilet as my eyes water and I try to recover.

"Jesus, Jess," Rosie's voice says. I turn to see her concerned face behind me. "Are you okay?"

"I'm fine," I say, wiping my mouth and heading to the sink to rinse it out with water. "Just been feeling a bit under the weather the past little while."

We walk back to the table in silence and sit down. The plate of waffles is still sitting untouched, and I feel my stomach churn again in warning. I push the plate away from me and take a long drink of water. When I put the glass down, I see Harper and Rosie exchange a glance.

"How long has this been going on?" Rosie asks slowly.

I shrug. "I don't know. A couple weeks?"

"A couple weeks?" Harper answers, her eyebrows shooting up toward her hairline.

I shrug again. "Yeah. It's no big deal, it usually passes in a few minutes and then I'm fine the rest of the day."

They look at each other again and I sigh. "What? Why are you guys looking at each other like that? What's going on?"

"Jess," Rosie says slowly, swinging her eyes to me. "When was the last time you got your period?"

"I, uh... a couple weeks ago. Wait, no. I'm..." I trail off. "I don't know. I can't remember."

"Is there any chance..." Harper starts slowly and looks at Rosie again. "Is there any chance you could be pregnant?"

"No," I answer quickly. "No! Definitely not. I haven't even had sex in two months! I've told you I'm having a dry spell."

"Right, but two months..."

The two of them look at me with concern drawn over their faces. I look down at my plate of waffles and gulp as I look back at them.

"How..." I shake my head. "No. It's not possible! How could that be possible?"

"Let's go to the pharmacy after breakfast," Rosie says. She turns to her pancakes and stabs them with a fork. Her voice sounds almost too casual when she speaks again. "We can pick up a test and just be sure. You're probably not pregnant, but it doesn't hurt to take a test."

"Yeah," Harper adds. "Just in case."

"Guys, I know you both got pregnant unexpectedly, but that doesn't mean it's a normal thing to happen. We used protection! We were careful!"

"So were we," Rosie says gently.

"Us too," Harper adds. "Let's just get the test."

I gulp and finally cut off a tiny bit of my waffles. "Fine," I say, bringing the food to my mouth. "But I don't really see the point."

Even as the words leave my mouth, I know that I don't believe them. Something in the way Rosie and Harper are looking at me tells me they already know what the test is going to show.

39

OWEN

Sam takes a deep breath and looks at the stack of tablecloths and boxes of streamers and centerpieces in the storage room.

"That should be everything," she says with a sigh.

I shut the door and lock it before putting the keys back in my pocket. "Great. What time did you say you'd be back tomorrow morning to start setting up?"

"My brother and a few others will be over around 8 a.m."

"I'll have the beers ready," I answer with a smile.

She laughs. "Just wait a couple hours, please. I'd like them to remember my wedding and for it to not get too messy."

"If you insist," I answer with a grin.

She thanks me and heads out the front entrance. I watch her leave and turn back to the closed storage room door. In twenty-four hours, Jess will be here, sitting at one of those tables. My heart starts to beat a bit faster and I almost jump out of my skin when my phone rings. I look at the screen and frown.

"Hi, Mom."

"Hi honey," she says. She sounds almost too friendly. "How's my favorite son doing?"

"I'm fine, mom. What's up?" She never calls me just to chat. There's always a reason or a request or a demand. Ever since my father got convicted of fraud, she's been particularly ruthless.

"When are you going to finish up with your little country project?" She asks.

"It's not a little country project, mom," I sigh. "I've renovated an entire hotel and started turning a profit within the first six months of re-opening."

"Of course you did, honey, and that's why I'm so proud of you."

I grunt in response and wait for her to tell me why she's calling.

"Your father wants you to come back to New York," she finally says.

"My father doesn't have control over where I go, and if my father wants me to come back why didn't he call me himself?"

"Oh, you know how busy he is with the trial and everything. Listen. You get a manager in because we need you at the company."

"I told you, mom, I'm not working for the company anymore. I won't be involved in it. I didn't know what kind of business you guys were doing, and I can't believe I didn't get convicted of anything. I won't be associated with it."

My heart is pounding and I know my voice sounds harsh. I can almost feel a wave of cold come through the phone with my mother's voice.

"Don't you forget where you came from, and who paid for that little hotel you're working in. Don't forget who made you what you are. You will come back, and you will work for your father. We need a clean name to put the new businesses to."

"Oh, right, so you just want to use me to start up some

other fucking sham of a business, except this time it'll be me who takes the fall if you get caught, is that it?"

There's no noise on the other end of the phone except for my mother's heavy breathing. She says nothing until I hear a click and the line goes dead. My heart is thumping in my chest as I look at the blank phone.

That's the first time I've stood up to her like that. I know how deep her anger runs, and I know I'll be in her bad books for a while but right now I just don't care. There's a wedding here tomorrow, the hotel is as busy as ever, and in less than twenty-four hours I'll be seeing the one woman that's been stuck in my mind for the past two months.

I take a deep breath and head up the stairs to my room. I toss my phone down on the table and turn to my dresser. I pull open the bottom drawer and take out a stack of files, putting them on the table next to my phone and opening them up.

I flick open the top file and run my eyes over the pages, flicking through them quickly. It's all still here. Every one of the transactions, every one of the false companies and inflated charges. The prosecution doesn't have any of this, and with one email I could destroy him. I only found these documents when I was clearing out my office and filing everything before I left, but it's all here. Every crime, in black and white.

I take a deep breath and close the files up again, sticking them under my arm. There's a big scanner in the office downstairs. I head down and take out a little black USB thumb drive. I stick it into my computer, and one by one, I start copying the files onto the device. Every time a file copies over, my heart thumps a bit harder in my chest.

When everything is done, I look at the little yellow folder on the screen. I right click the folder and type in a password for extra protection. I stick the paper files back in their folder and jog up the stairs to store them safely in the bottom drawer. The USB drive goes onto my key ring and I slide it into my pocket, tapping the keys with my hand as I try to slow my heartbeat down.

These files were always supposed to be a safety net when I left New York, in case I was accused of anything else. I always told myself I'd never use them, that I'd protect my parents with my life. But now, I'm starting to realize that they don't feel the same way about me. If my mother decides to make me the scapegoat for their next scummy business, I might have to turn against my own family.

40

JESS

I'M NUMB. The whole trip from New York to Lexington is a blur, because all I can think about is the two little blue lines on the six different pregnancy tests I've taken since breakfast yesterday.

At first, I was in denial. I couldn't believe it. By the fourth pregnancy test I started getting angry. Now, as I make my way up the path to Gram's house, I just feel empty.

I'm pregnant.

For the second time in my life, I've gotten pregnant by accident. For the second time in my life, I'm completely alone for it.

When this happened when I was a teenager, I was confused and terrified and ashamed. Now I'm confused and terrified but I'm not ashamed. I can already feel my love growing for the baby, and something else is growing inside me. It feels like fierceness or determination, or just a singular focus to give this baby the best life it could possibly have. I don't know how I'll do it, but I know I will.

Gram opens the door and wraps me in a hug, and I still feel numb except for that tiny fire burning inside me.

"You didn't have to stay up, Gram," I say. "You should have gone to bed."

"Don't be silly, Jessica," she answers. "It's only nine o'clock."

She's wearing her dressing gown as she helps me into the house. I head upstairs to my room and say goodnight to Gram. She hugs me in the doorway and I melt into her arms. Right now, I wish I was still a little girl and she could wrap her arms around me and make it all better. She pulls away and strokes her finger along my cheek.

"Beautiful girl," she says softly. "You know I love you with all my heart, right?"

I force a smile. "Of course, Gram. I love you too."

"I just want you to be happy."

"I am happy," I respond softly. It sounds fake even to my ears. Gram nods slowly and smiles. Her wrinkles look even deeper than last time, and her eyes are just a little bit cloudy. She takes a deep breath and smiles again.

"Okay. See you tomorrow." She turns toward her room and I close the door and fall onto my bed, staring at the ceiling.

It seems like I always end up here, in this room, staring at the same ceiling and thinking about my whole world being turned upside down. Now, for the second time, I'm wondering how I ended up pregnant and single.

Are you going to tell him?

Harper's question rings in my ears and I try to remember the details of Owen's face. The thought of seeing him after not speaking for two months makes me more nervous than I want to admit. The thought of seeing him and telling him that I'm pregnant with his child is completely terrifying.

Eventually, I fall into a fitful sleep. I wake up a few times in the night, tossing and turning as I think about what tomorrow will bring.

Will he be there? What will I say to him? I can't say anything at Sam's wedding, the day should be about her. I'll have to wait until after.

Finally, the first grey light of dawn starts to appear and I sit up in bed. I know I won't sleep anymore, so I put on my running shoes and slip out the door. The air is fresh and clean as I start to run.

Before I know it, I'm rounding the corner toward the clearing. I take a deep breath and duck through the trees, coming to a stop by the river. The rock is still there, overhanging the bank where Owen and I sat and talked and I told him everything.

My eyes sweep around and I remember the way he held me when we made love, and the way he looked into my eyes and held my hand.

I've never had anyone look at me like that before.

Is it really that bad if he was accused of fraud? The charges were thrown out, after all. I glance at the trees as the leaves rustle back and forth and then glance up at the sky. There aren't any clouds to look at today, so I let my eyes rest on the flowing river.

I take a deep breath. I was upset that I had opened up to him like never before and he didn't return the favor. And then when I confronted him, he said those awful things to me. The memories of that conversation start flooding my mind and I turn back to the path.

He obviously didn't care about me, if he would believe that I'd sleep my way into college. If he believed things that Mary Hanson said the minute I left even after I told him how she treated me, then he's clearly not the type of man that will stand by my side through thick and thin.

My hand floats to my stomach and I run my fingers in a slow circle over it. At the end of the day, it's just me and this baby. If Owen wants to be a part of the baby's life, that's great, but he's shown himself to be untrustworthy. I won't have my child be influenced by someone like that.

As my resolve sets, I start to jog back toward Gram's house. I'll tell him about the baby, but I'll be very clear that whatever happened between us two months ago is over. I don't need or want him in my life.

I repeat those words to myself with every stride until it's like a mantra. I don't want or need him in my life. By the time I get back to Gram's house, I almost believe myself. Just when I'm about to turn to the front door, I hesitate and veer off in the other direction. My heart starts pounding in my chest as I turn down the road to Main Street, and toward the Lexington Hotel.

41

OWEN

SHE'S IN TOWN SOMEWHERE, probably at her grandmother's house. I haven't slept a wink last night, and I know it's because I'm nervous.

I'm nervous about seeing her, and talking to her, and trying to tell her that I'm sorry. I'm nervous that she won't let me speak to her, and that I'll be left with this weight on my chest for the rest of my life.

Ever since that conversation on the phone, it's like I haven't been able to breathe properly. It's like every time I try to take a deep breath, there's something wrapped around my torso that stops me from inhaling completely. I feel trapped in my own body, and today the weight feels ten times heavier.

I rub my eyes and sit up in bed. I won't sleep any more, I know it. There's lots to do to set up and make sure the day goes smoothly, so I might as well get started. I pull on a pair of jeans and an old black tee-shirt. I can change into my suit later.

The old stairs creak as I jog downstairs and start the coffee machine behind the bar. Joe won't be in for a few hours, so I get to work restocking the fridges with drinks. I move methodically from one fridge to the next. Sam's family have delivered six cases of champagne and I shake my head as I transfer them to the fridge. It's going to be a party.

By the time I'm done stocking the fridges, my coffee is ready. I fill up a mug and take the cup out to the front of the hotel. There's a rocking chair on the end of the porch, and it's been my morning ritual to have a coffee and read the paper out there. I've definitely embraced the small town life.

I settle into the chair and take a sip of coffee. It's strong and bitter and exactly what I want. I'll need more than one cup to get me through today.

Just as I'm bringing the mug to my lips a second time, I hear footsteps running down the sidewalk. I frown and check my watch, wondering who would be out at this hour. It's only six in the morning.

I wait as the seconds tick by and the footsteps come closer. Soon, the runner will come into view. I rock gently back and forth, bringing my mug to my lips once more. The coffee touches my lips and suddenly the runner comes around the corner, flying toward the front of the hotel.

Her brown hair is swinging back and forth with every step. Her strides are graceful and it almost feels like time slows down. My jaw drops just as her eyes scan the hotel. She spots me. My coffee mug, forgotten in my hand, keeps tilting toward my lips until the burning hot liquid pours down my chin and onto my lap.

"Ah, damn it!" I yell, jumping up and brushing my pants as if it would stop the coffee from seeping in.

Her laugh is the first thing I hear, and it sends an arrow straight through my chest. I glance up as Jess slows to a stop in front of me, tilting her chin to look up at me from the sidewalk. I'm standing on the porch, with just a couple feet and the white bannister between us. Her chest is heaving up and down as she pants from her run, with a smile still lingering on her lips.

Time stops as we stare at each other. She's more beautiful than I remembered. Her eyes are just as piercing, but her features are more defined than I remember. I can't speak. Even if I could, I wouldn't be able to think of anything to say. She breaks the spell between us when she tilts her head to the side and speaks.

"You okay?"

"Yeah, I'm fine. You just surprised me."

"Oh so it's my fault, is it," she asks with a grin, taking a step toward the porch. "Don't blame me for your clumsiness."

"I don't blame you for anything," I breathe. She looks at me curiously and then glances down at the low shrubs lining the front of the hotel. She clears her throat.

"Garden looks good."

"Thanks. Your grandma has been a big help."

"She likes you," she says as her eyes sweep up to mine.

"I like her too," I respond. I wish I could think of something more interesting to say, but all I can do is look at her and breathe. I'm afraid if I say anything wrong or if I make a sudden movement she might disappear into thin air. She falls silent again and kicks a pebble near her foot. She runs a hand over her hair, smoothing it down toward her pony tail before taking a deep breath.

When her eyes lift up to me again there's something in them that I don't recognize. She looks more determined than I've ever seen her. She looks almost cold as her lips part and she inhales one last time before she speaks.

"I'm pregnant."

42
JESS

THAT WASN'T EXACTLY how I'd intended on telling him, but here we are. It's as good a way as any, I guess. My heart is hammering against my ribcage and I'm not sure if it's because of the run or if it's because of what I just told him.

He's staring at me, wide-eyed and slack-jawed, his mug of coffee dangerously close to spilling on the ground again.

"It's yours," I add.

He closes his mouth and then opens it again, looks at the ground and then back at me.

"I..." he stops. "What?"

"I don't know," I say with a shrug. "I just found out yesterday.

"Are you..." he trails off and sits back down in his chair, dropping his forehead into his hand and setting the mug of coffee on his knee. I wring my hands together as I watch him. Maybe I shouldn't have said it like that.

Even through the shock he still looks good. He runs his fingers through his hair in that familiar motion of his and I wish I could walk up to him and tangle my own fingers into his hair. I wish he would lean his forehead against mine and tell me how much he cares about me. I wish I could press my lips against his and feel his hands on me, and then run my fingers over every muscle in his body.

Everything inside me is screaming to walk over to him, to jump the shrub if I have to, but my feet stay rooted to the ground. He looks back at me and takes a deep breath.

"Are you sure?"

"About being pregnant? Or about it being yours?"

"Both, I guess."

"Well I haven't been to the doctor yet, but I did take six pregnancy tests," I admit. "And you're the only guy I've had sex with, so…"

He nods and takes another breath. He shakes his head slowly.

"You know, when I thought about you coming here, I thought about what I would say. I had this whole speech planned out where I would apologize for all the things I said and I'd tell you everything about my father's company and the trial."

He thought about me? He wanted to talk to me? My heart grows in my chest and I take a step closer to him until my thighs are brushing against the shrub. He glances back at me and shakes his head again.

"I didn't think we would be having this conversation. Not in a million years."

"Neither did I," I admit.

We stand there quietly for what seems like an eternity. I don't know what to say. He has his head in his hand again and I don't know what he's thinking. Finally he lifts his head to look at me.

"What's your plan? With the baby, I mean."

"What do you mean?" My eyes narrow as I watch him struggle to find the words.

"Well, what were you thinking of doing?"

"What are you asking me, Owen," I say. His name sounds weird in my mouth. I used to love saying his name but now it tastes bitter. "Are you asking me if I'm keeping the baby?"

We stare at each other in silence and the beating in my heart turns hollow as the anger and outrage start to build inside me. Before he has a chance to answer, I turn around and start running toward Gram's house.

It's lucky that I've travelled this route about a million times, because my eyes are completely blurred by tears. My feet hit the pavement and send a jolt through my body with every step as I try to hold myself together.

I don't know what I expected, but I expected more than that. I can tell myself that I'm okay on my own, that I don't want or need him, but I didn't think it would hurt quite that much to see the panic in his eyes.

I was prepared to do it on my own but now I realize that I was holding on to some stupid, naive fantasy that he'd wrap me in his arms and we'd walk into the sunset together.

He doesn't want me, and he doesn't want the baby. I am on my own. I knew I was on my own before, but the reality of what that means is just starting to show itself to me. I'm on my own. I'm alone.

I push the door open and rush upstairs, jumping in the shower as soon as I can get my clothes off. I shouldn't have gone to him this morning. Now I have to spend all day at the Lex, pretending to be happy for my oldest friend as she marries the love of her life.

I have to pretend to be happy for her, and I have to pretend that my heart hasn't just been ripped out of my chest.

Once again, I'm crying in the shower over a guy I barely know. Once again, I have to pull myself together and watch yet another friend finds happiness while all I've found is loneliness and heartbreak.

I wallow in my self-pity until the hot water runs out and the shower turns ice-cold. I stand under the cold stream until my body stiffens. With a shake of the head, I reach down to turn it off.

Pull yourself together.

This isn't me. I'm on my own, but I always have been. Nothing has changed. I still have this baby growing inside me, and I'm still going to love it with every fiber of my being. I'm going to go to this wedding, and I'm going to be happy for my friend. I'm going to celebrate two people being in love and I won't think about myself.

I straighten myself up and take a deep breath. I can do this.

43

OWEN

I can't do this. I can't spend all day in the same building as her, let alone the same room. I can't plaster a smile on my face and pretend to be happy for Sam and Ronnie when I've just heard that I'm going to be a dad.

I still can't believe it.

I sit on the edge of my bed and stare at the coffee stain on my jeans. I'm in a daze. Finally, I pull the bedside table drawer open. I find the old box of condoms and stare at it. Jess was the only person I used these with.

"You had one job," I say to the box. "One fucking job."

I shake my head and turn the box over. I frown as my eyes catch some stamped writing on the bottom corner.

Best before: 01/2017

My heart starts thumping as I read the letters over and over. 2017? These condoms have been expired for over a year?

"Fuck, fuck, fuck!" I whisper as I flip the box over and back in my hands. "Fuck!"

I knew I hadn't slept with anyone in a long time, but I

hadn't realized how long. I toss the box across the floor and put my head in my hands.

As soon as she told me she was pregnant, I knew it was mine. I could tell by the way she looked at me, but if there was any doubt it's gone now. I can't believe I've been using condoms that have been expired over a year.

I stand up and take a deep breath before putting my hands to my eyes and rubbing them. I sit back down and stand up again, and then turn around in a circle.

I don't know what I'm doing. I don't know what I'm supposed to do. How do people react to this?

I'm freaking out.

There's a knock on the door and I jump. Joe's voice comes through the door.

"Boss,"

"Yeah!" I call out, trying my best to sound normal.

"Wedding set up crew is here."

"All right, I'll be right down."

I think I hear him grunt through the door and his heavy footsteps shuffle down the hall. I go to the bathroom and splash some water on my face and then look at myself in the mirror. It looks like I've aged about ten years since yesterday.

I pat my face dry and take a deep breath before heading downstairs. I can hear the voices from the landing upstairs, and with another deep inhalation I make my way down.

"Owen!" Sam calls out. "This is Maggie. She's going to be in charge of the set up."

"Hi Maggie," I say, extending my hand. The older woman shakes it firmly and nods.

"Right," she says. "We need those tables set up in the main hall. And you," she points at me. "Get those tablecloths. Where are the lights?"

Within minutes, the whole ground floor of the hotel is a

flurry of activity. Normally I'd find it difficult to have someone else order me around but right now I relish it. I do exactly as she says and I turn my brain off. My body goes into autopilot as I help haul tables, chairs, I tack up strings of lights, I arrange flowers and centerpieces.

The morning flies by and pretty soon, the Lexington Hotel Bar is completely transformed.

"Doesn't even look like the same place," I breathe as I look around the room. Sam's brother Cory chuckles.

"It's amazing what some tablecloths and Christmas lights will do to a place, huh?"

"Looks almost classy in here," I laugh.

"Almost," he says. "What do you say we crack a couple cold ones?"

"Not a minute too soon," I say. "First one's on the house." I reach behind the bar and grab a few beers. As soon as the bitter liquid hits my tongue, I feel my shoulders relax.

For the first time since I saw Jess this morning, I start thinking that maybe I *can* do this. I can make it through the day if I just put one foot in front of the other and try not to think about the huge, looming reality that in a few short months I'm going to be a dad.

44

JESS

My cheeks hurt from plastering this smile on my face all day. If there was ever a day in my life that I didn't want a gaggle of people around me messing with my hair, my makeup, and a million cameras in my face, today would be that day.

If I had my choice, I would be curled up in bed with the curtains drawn and the lights off and I wouldn't get up for three days. If I had a choice, I would eat nothing but ice cream and chocolate until my stomach hurt.

If I had a choice, I wouldn't be pregnant.

As soon as the thought crosses my mind, I sit up straighter. It surprises me because it's not true. As much as Owen's reaction hurt me, as much as I'd rather be having a kid when I'm in a stable relationship, as much as I am terrified of what will happen, I *want* this baby.

I want to be a mom.

The first real smile I've had in two days floats onto my lips and a camera flashes. I blink a couple times and Sam laughs.

"Come on, Jess. Church time. I'm getting myself my very own husband."

The second real smile of the day splits my lips and I wrap Sam in a hug.

"Congratulations, Sam," I say as we embrace. She squeezes me a bit tighter and then pushes me off.

"You're going to mess up this hair," she says with a laugh, patting the sides of her head.

"You look gorgeous," I smile. "Let's go."

THE CEREMONY IS BEAUTIFUL. I dab at the corners of my eyes with a tissue and try to ignore the tightening in my chest. The way Sam and Ronnie look at each other is impossible to ignore. As soon as he hears the words, Ronnie dips Sam backward and plants a kiss on her lips. Everyone in the church cheers and claps as the two of them laugh and turn to the congregation. Sam glances at me and I finally just let the tears flow free.

My two oldest friends are married, and I can honestly say I couldn't be happier for them. This morning, I didn't think I'd be able to make it through the day but right now all that matters is the way their arms are locked around each other and the way Ronnie's leaning down to whisper in her ear. Sam laughs and I can almost feel the love radiating off them.

"Come on," Sam calls out. "Let's go to the Lex!"

And with those seven words, the warmth in my heart turns to ice. The part of the day that I've been dreading is here, and I'm going to have to face Owen.

I shuffle behind Sam and paint the fake smile on my face again. My grandmother finds me and hooks her arm into mine, squeezing my bicep in her hand.

"What's that sad look, Jessica? You haven't been yourself since you got here."

"It's nothing, Gram. Just tired."

"I know when you're tired, honey, and this isn't it."

The two of us walk slowly and she turns her head to look at me.

"When I met your grandfather," she starts all of a sudden, "I thought he was the most rude, arrogant man I'd ever met. I didn't want anything to do with him."

"I thought it was love at first sight! That's what you always said."

Gram chuckles and shakes her head. "He was walking around town like he owned the place and I wanted none of it. It wasn't until I got to know him and I saw the type of man he was that I fell in love with him."

She pats my arm gently and goes quiet as we walk down Main Street toward the big hotel.

"Sometimes you need to give people a second chance," she says. I glance over at her but she keeps her eyes straight forward. My heart squeezes in my chest and I try to swallow but there's a lump in my throat.

"Gram," I say. "I don't know if it's that simple."

"When you get to my age, you'll realize that sometimes it is that simple. You have to open up sometimes when you don't want to. I love you, Jessica."

"I love you too, Gram."

There's a hurricane of emotions inside me, but all I can do is walk slowly with my grandmother toward the father of my unborn child, and pretend like everything is okay. Gram pats my arm gently and we walk the rest of the way in silence.

45

OWEN

I HEAR the voices from the wedding guests as I'm hanging up the last set of lights around the bar. The first guests start to drift in and pretty soon the whole place is packed. I scan the room for her, but she isn't here yet.

What if she decided not to come?

Maggie, the wedding planner, leans over to me and points to the PA system.

"Is this ready?"

I nod. She says nothing, but pulls out her phone and says a few words. The lights in the bar dim, and a spotlight appears, pointing toward the door. I glance up at the light and frown. I hadn't even realized that had been installed today. I must be completely out of it.

The light shines at the door and the wedding party starts to come through. Two by two, the bridesmaids and groomsmen step through. My heart starts to thump as I see Jess come into view. She's arm-in-arm with Sam's brother Cory.

She looks radiant. She's wearing the same dress as the

other bridesmaids but somehow it looks better on her. It's dark blue and floor-length, cinched at the waist and flowing all around her. She looks like an angel.

Jess scans the room and for a brief second our eyes meet. There are ten thousand things in her eyes and in that instant, time stops. All that exists is Jess, and me. She looks at me and I feel the pain in her eyes, I see the loneliness and the fear and my heart shatters into a million pieces.

I've been an idiot.

She glances away and forces a smile onto her face. I keep looking at her, hoping she'll glance my way, hoping she'll give me even half a second of her attention, but she turns to the door and claps as Sam and Ron make their entrance.

Every single person is clapping and shouting, all eyes are on Sam and Ron. I'm sure they can hear us three towns over.

I clap along with everyone, but my eyes stay glued on Jess. I can see her profile as she welcomes Sam and Ron into the Lex. She dips her head down and I stare at the curve of her neck, and the way her hair cascades down her back. She claps her hands and I watch the way every move is graceful, the way she turns toward Sam as she walks by to the head table.

Jess follows Sam and takes a seat to her right. I finally rip my eyes away from her and turn around, ducking into the office and closing the door.

I let out all the air from my lungs and flop down onto my office chair. In front of me is the chair she sat in the first day we met. Right there is the glass that she drank from, and there's the whiskey we shared. I haven't touched it since she left.

I rub my temples and take a deep breath. Maybe it's time for me to drink something a bit stronger.

The golden liquid shines in the glass when I hold it up

before pouring it all down my throat. It burns as it goes down and I close my eyes and savor the sensation. At least it feels like something. All day I've been numb, and now I feel like a hand is gripping my heart and squeezing as hard as possible. The whiskey burns but at least it takes my mind off everything else for even just a second.

Jess obviously doesn't want to talk to me today. She turned away the minute our eyes met and has avoided my gaze since she got in. Why didn't I go to her this morning? Why didn't I hug her, or tell her I'd be there for our child? Why did I stay where I was like that? Of course she doesn't want to talk to me, she thinks I want nothing to do with her or the kid!

I pour some more alcohol into the glass when there's a soft knock on the door. I sigh and put my glass down, putting the cap back on the green bottle of whiskey.

"Come in," I sigh.

The door opens slowly and I almost fall backward when I see her blue flowing dress step through the door. She closes it behind her and takes a deep breath as she looks me in the eye.

"Jess," I breathe.

"Owen," she replies.

We're quiet for a few seconds. Once again, I wish I knew what to say. There are so many things flying through my mind and all I want to do is tell her that I care about her, that I care about the baby, that I'll be there for her.

Something in the way she's looking at me stops me. There's a hardness in her eyes.

"We left on a bad note today," she starts. "That was my fault. I shouldn't have run away and I probably could have told you about the baby more... diplomatically."

"It wasn't your fault," I say, shaking my head. She holds up her hand and I stop talking.

"I just want you to know that I am not expecting anything from you. I'm prepared to raise this baby by myself, but I just wanted to tell you that I'm keeping it. Nothing you can say or do will change my mind."

My heart starts thumping. I can't help it—a smile starts to spread across my face. Jess frowns.

"What?"

"I just," I start. "I'm just happy to hear that."

"Hear what? That you're off the hook?" Her voice is hard and I shake my head, standing up and taking a step toward her. She bristles and takes a step back. I pause.

"No," I say gently. "I'm happy that you want to keep the baby... Our baby." The last two words come out barely above a whisper. Her eyes narrow and she searches my face. She looks suspicious.

"I thought you didn't want me to have it," she says slowly.

"I was just in shock, Jess," I say, holding out my hand. "This isn't what I was expecting but it doesn't mean it's a bad thing."

Her shoulders relax down a fraction of an inch and she nods.

"I should probably get back," she says, nodding to the door. "Maybe we can talk about this later?"

I dip my chin down. "Yeah. Of course."

She nods again and turns to the door. Her hand slips onto the doorknob and she glances back at me. The first hint of a smile appears on her lips.

"Thanks."

There's a lump in my throat so all I can do is nod as tears start prickling the corners of my eyes. She slips out the door and I slump back into my chair, letting all the breath out of my lungs. I look at the glass of whiskey on my desk and take a tiny sip. Somehow it tastes sweeter than it did a few minutes ago.

46

JESS

THERE'S the tiniest sliver of hope inside me as I walk back to the table. I sit next to Sam and my heart feels lighter. My smile comes easier as I lean toward her and touch my shoulder to hers.

She turns to me and smiles.

"I'm happy for you, Sam," I say.

She grins. "Finally."

"What's that supposed to mean!"

Sam laughs. "You've been sulking all day." A bolt of guilt passes through my stomach and Sam laughs. "It's okay, Jess. As long as you're happy now. Your fake smile sucks, by the way."

For the first time today, I start laughing. Sam grins and finally starts laughing with me until the tears start gathering in my eyes. I dab them away with a tissue and she shakes her head.

"I'll explain later," I finally say.

"You don't need to explain anything, Jess. Just be happy today."

I nod, and this time the tears in my eyes aren't from

laughing. She squeezes my arm before grabbing her glass of champagne. She clinks it against mine and takes a sip. I bring the glass to my lips and pretend to drink, but put it back down without having any. I put a hand to my stomach and stroke it gently before turning my attention back to the table.

The wedding is beautiful. There's speeches and tears and laughter, and I'm in awe of how good a simple wedding in the town's hotel can be. Pretty soon everyone is up and dancing on the dance floor, waiting for the fourth of July fireworks to start. Other patrons start drifting into the hotel and mixing with the wedding until it seems like the whole town is in this tiny room.

I'm standing at the edge of the dance floor when Owen appears beside me. His arm brushes against mine and I can immediately smell that fresh, manly scent that I've missed so much. It's the closest we've been since I left Lexington two months ago, and my whole body starts to feel electric.

He leans his mouth close to my ear.

"You look beautiful," he whispers. I duck my chin and smile, trying to hide my blush. Even those simple words send a thrill down my spine as my center starts to heat up. He holds out his hand and nods to the dance floor.

I can't help it, a smile breaks across my face. I slip my fingers into his palm and he guides me out onto the dance floor just as the music starts to slow down. His hand finds the small of my back and I feel like my whole body is trembling. His cheek rests against mine and we sway, chest to chest.

"I missed you," he growls into my ear. The flame inside me grows hotter as my heart starts to beat.

"I missed you too," I answer. My voice is barely above a whisper.

"Whatever we have, whatever this thing is between us," he says. "I want to keep going."

I pull my head back. "Is that why you knocked me up?" I ask with an eyebrow raised. He laughs, throwing his head back. I can't help but smile as well.

"My master plan is working," he says with a grin. His eyes soften and he shakes his head. "I'm fucking terrified."

"So am I," I answer. He smiles and holds me a bit closer.

We sway back and forth on the dance floor for an eternity. I don't even know if we're moving to the beat of the music. I can't even hear the music. All I hear is his heartbeat and mine, inches apart from each other. I forget where I am and who is around. I forget everything except the feeling of his hand on my back, his cheek against mine and my fingers on his palm.

I lift my hands up and wrap them around his neck, putting my forehead against his. He slides both hands onto the small of my back and a sigh shudders through me. As much as I don't want to let my guard down, as much as I'm afraid that he'll change his mind and walk away, as much as I'm terrified of having this child, right now, I'm happy.

Right now I could stay like this, swaying gently side to side forever.

The music ends and everyone on the dance floor starts clapping. Reluctantly, I pull myself away from Owen and clap. We look at each other for a moment and he winks at me before starting to clap.

I see movement out of the corner of my eye and turn to see Mary Hanson in the doorway. She's staring at me with laser focus. A chill runs down my spine. Owen glances at me and follows my gaze. He brushes his hand on the small of my back and leans into me.

"You okay?"

"I'm fine," I say, turning to him. He looks at me and smiles. For a moment, I think that he might be about to kiss me. His eyes soften and he turns his chest toward mine. He puts his hands on my hips and his lips part ever so slightly. Just as his chin starts to dip down, that fake-sweet voice rings out beside us.

"Well look at you two lovebirds," Mary says.

We both jump and turn to her. She grins at me.

"Owen, Jess," she says, nodding to each of us in turn. "I'd like to introduce you to my fiancé. Jess, I believe you already know him."

A man steps out from behind her and my jaw drops. "Michael?"

"Hi, Jess," he says, glancing at me and smiling shyly. I feel Owen stiffen beside me.

"I thought you said you didn't know Mary's fiancé," he says to me gently. I can hear an edge to his voice that wasn't there before. Mary's smile widens as she puts her arm around Michael's waist.

I'm still in shock. My eyes flick from Mary to Michael and back to Mary again.

"Oh she knows him, don't you, Jess?"

I nod. Michael is still looking at me, and he glances quickly at Owen. I gulp. "Good to see you again," I lie.

Michael nods. "You too."

My heart is thumping and I glance around. I need to get away. "Excuse me," I say as I turn and almost run to the bathroom. It's not until I'm inside that I let out a huge breath and lean on the counter.

Michael, my first boyfriend. The guy who left me pregnant and alone. *That's* Mary's fiancé?

47

OWEN

JESS HURRIES to the bathroom and I turn back to the couple.

"Congratulations on your upcoming wedding," I say stiffly. They both nod, and Mary smiles.

"Thank you, Owen. I'm glad you two finally got to meet."

"Me too. If you'll excuse me, I think Joe needs some help behind the bar." Not a moment too soon, I slip away. I glance over at the bathrooms. What the hell is going on? Why did Jess run away? Why did she tell me she didn't know Mary's fiancé if she obviously does?

The questions are flying around my head, and the peacefulness in my heart that I felt with Jess in my arms on the dance floor has evaporated. Instead, all I have is uncertainty, doubt, and a million questions.

Jess has disappeared and I keep scanning the room for her. Where did she go? I walk around the room and finally spot her, leaning against the wall in the back corner.

"Where did you go?" I ask. She turns her head toward me and then looks down at the ground.

"I didn't feel like talking to her."

"Who's that guy? Her fiancé? I thought you said you didn't

know him." My voice sounds harsher than I intended, and Jess flinches. Her hand goes up to her stomach and I take a step toward her.

"I said I didn't know who he was. I didn't realize it was him."

"Who is he?" I ask more gently.

Her face sours and she shakes her head. The frustration starts to build inside me. Jess won't look at me and I glance around the room again. I make eye contact with Mary, who's staring at the two of us intently.

I take a deep breath and try to soften my voice. "Jess, please tell me? I hate to see you like this. I want.... I want to be there for you."

Jess finally lifts her eyes up to mine and I see deep-rooted pain in them. She swallows and then opens her lips to speak.

"He was my first boyfriend. The one that I... the one who left." *The one who got you pregnant, you mean.* "I don't even know why I'm upset. I haven't spoken to him in over a decade. I don't know, just seeing him here, with Mary, when Sam and Ronnie are getting married and I'm just pregnant by accident again, it's just," she sobs and her hands fly up to her face.

I wrap my arms around her and hold her close to me. She's shaking, and I just hold her and make wordless soothing noises until her body softens and she relaxes. Her arms slowly wrap themselves around me until she pulls away and brushes a tear away from her eye.

"Sorry," she says. "This is just too much for me. I don't know how I'm supposed to feel."

I laugh. "Neither do I." I brush her hair off her face and wipe another tear away. "We'll figure it out, Jess. I'm happy you're here."

She finally smiles and my heart starts to grow. "It's good to see you."

"Good to see you too."

Jess glances across the room and frowns. "Gram looks tired. I might have to take her home."

"I'll drive her," I say.

She looks at me sideways and shakes her head. "I saw you downing that whiskey earlier," she laughs. "I haven't been drinking."

"All right," I answer. "You'll come back after?"

"If you want me to," she answers with a grin.

"I want you to."

The smile on her face makes my heart melt as she squeezes my hand and slips away toward her grandmother. I watch her put her arm around the old woman and help her to her feet. The two of them head to Sam and Ronnie and then over to the entrance. I watch every movement, unable to take my eyes off her.

Even seeing her take care of her grandmother like that makes my heart swell. She's going to be a great mother.

"So, you guys are an item now, or what?"

I turn to the voice and see Mary leaning on her hip with her head tilted to the side. She licks her lips slowly and raises an eyebrow. I shrug.

"I'm not sure what we are."

Mary narrows her eyes and smiles at me. The smile doesn't seem to change her face at all except for her lips, giving her an eerie sort of expression. "Hey, Owen, I think there was a problem with my last paycheck. Do you mind if we have a look at it?"

Is she pouting right now? Is that supposed to be cute?

"How about tomorrow," I answer, shifting my gaze to the party.

"I'd really rather sort it out now," she says. I glance at her and sigh. I'm not going to get rid of her until that's done.

"All right," I say, gesturing to the office. "Let's go in here and have a look."

She smiles the same way and nods before turning around and swaying her way to the office. If she wasn't so good behind the bar, I'd have let her go a long time ago.

48

JESS

"Thank you, honey. You get back over there now," Gram says as I help her up the stairs. I can almost feel her tiredness as she moves slowly, dragging one foot forward after the next.

I say nothing, instead I just help her walk to her bedroom. I help her take off her jacket and put her jewelry away while she goes to the bathroom and changes into her dressing gown. She comes back out and sits on the bed, letting out a big sigh. Finally, she shifts her gaze up to me and smiles.

"He likes you, you know."

"Who?" I ask, pretending to be confused. Gram chuckles.

"Mr. McAllister. Remember what I said before, Jessica. Some things are worth fighting for. He's a nice man."

"You're just worried I'll end up all alone," I laugh as I help her back into bed. Gram chuckles softly and lays her head on the pillow.

"I'm worried you'll end up unhappy." A lump forms in my throat and Gram takes my hand. "I'm proud of you, Jess. Always have been. You've turned out to be an independent, intelligent young woman and I couldn't ask for a better granddaughter. You'll make a wonderful mother one day."

I still can't speak and Gram smiles. In another breath she's asleep and I tiptoe out the door. It's a quiet drive back as I think about Gram's words. These past couple days she's been saying a lot of things to me about happiness and love. What is she trying to say, really? What would she say if she knew I was pregnant?

Maybe happiness is possible for me, and she sees me trying to push it away. Maybe I should just trust Owen, and trust that he wants to be with me and he wants this baby. Maybe I should let myself go and let my walls down and let him in. By the time I get back to the Lex, the party is in full swing. It's almost too loud after the silence of Gram's house.

I scan the room, looking for Owen. My heart feels light as I walk around.

I'm ready.

For the first time in my life, I'm ready to let happiness in. I'm ready to trust Owen and to open up to him and let him in. I'm ready to hear his story and I'm ready to accept that he's not a criminal. Maybe it is possible that he's as wonderful and caring as he seems. I'm ready to fall in love with him.

My thoughts surprise me. After spending all day trying to force my lips to curl upward, now I can't seem to stop smiling.

"Jess!"

I turn to see Michael walking toward me. The lightness in my heart feels dampened as soon as I see him. He offers me a beer and I shake my head.

"Thanks, not tonight," I say.

He nods and takes a sip of his own beer. He glances at the floor and then back up at me. It doesn't seem like he's going to say anything, so I start.

"So, you and Mary, huh?"

"Yeah," he says, nodding. "We've known each other for years and it just made sense."

Doesn't make sense to me.

"That's great, Michael, I'm happy for you. Now if you'll excuse me—"

"Wait, Jess," he says, holding his hand out. I pause, turning back to him. His eyes plead with me and he continues. "I just wanted to apologize. The way I treated you, leaving you after you..."

"Got pregnant."

"Right. Got pregnant. It was wrong."

I nod. "Okay. Thanks."

He shakes his head. "I mean, I'm sorry. I was a dumb kid. I freaked out and I left and I should have been there for you."

"What about shacking up with Mary two weeks after we found out I was pregnant? Was that just you 'freaking out'?" I hate the bitterness in my voice but I can't help it. His face contorts and he looks away. Finally, he swings his eyes back to mine.

"I'm sorry," he says again.

I realize my shoulders are tense and I relax them. I force my face to relax and I nod, and finally smile. I don't need to hold on to this anger. It's in the past. As I look at the guilt in Michael's face, I finally let go of it all.

"Thank you," I finally say. "It's okay. We were kids. It's probably for the best now."

Michael glances up at me hopefully, and when he sees the sincerity in my eyes he starts to smile. "Really?"

"Really. Water under the bridge."

His smile widens and I grin before sweeping the room with another look. "Thank you for apologizing. Hey, have you seen Owen?"

"No. I've been looking for Mary too, I saw her talking to him but I haven't seen either of them in ages."

I frown and glance back at him. He shrugs and takes a sip

of beer. My heart starts pounding and I glance at the bar and back around the room. There's no sign of him or Mary. Finally my eyes rest on the office door and my heart starts thumping even harder.

"In there," I manage to croak, nodding at the door. Michael shrugs and I start walking to the closed door. I don't understand why I'm suddenly nervous, but every step makes my whole body tremble a little bit more, and pretty soon all I can hear is the heartbeat rushing through my ears and all I can see is that closed door.

49

OWEN

"I don't see anything wrong with this paycheck, Mary," I sigh, leaning back in my chair. "Here are the hours you've worked, here's the schedule. We've cross-checked everything."

Mary sits on the desk and leans against her palms, dangling her feet in front of her. She pushes her chest out and looks me up and down.

"I must have made a mistake," she purrs.

I try not to roll my eyes. "Okay, well, next time just double check before you ask me about it, okay? I should get back outside." *Jess will be back any minute and I don't want to waste any more time in here with you.*

"What's the rush?" She asks as she slides off the desk. She moves her hands to the arms of the chair and leans toward me. "It's so loud out there, and it's so quiet in here."

"What are you doing," I say, looking away from her. "Stop, Mary, get off me."

She moves her hand to my cheek and before I know what's happening her face is moving toward mine. Before her lips can touch mine, I put my hand between us and push her face back until she stumbles backward.

I jump up and away as she yelps.

There's another noise, like a gasp at the doorway. I see a hint of movement and turn my head to see Mary's fiancé in the doorway. He's wide-eyed, staring at Mary as she gains her footing and follows my gaze to the door.

"He came onto me! He pushed himself on me!" She yells, pointing her finger at me. I make a gargled noise as I try to protest.

Michaels' face is dark as he continues to stare at her. Finally he turns slowly and walks to the exit. Mary rushes after him, still yelling lies about me. I rub my forehead and get up slowly, following them out of the office. They've carved a path through the crowd, with Mary still yelling as Michael walks away.

I look a bit further just to see Jess in the doorway. She's glancing over her shoulder and our eyes meet for a second. In them I see pain and betrayal, and my stomach drops as I realize that the movement I saw in the doorway wasn't Michael. It was her. She ducks out the door and disappears.

Suddenly I'm sprinting. I'm pushing people aside as I try to make my way to the exit. It seems like there are people everywhere—legs, arms, bodies, it's like moving through molasses.

"Wait! Jess!"

The whole wedding has stopped and people are staring first at Mary and Michael, and then at me as I try to run toward the exit. I finally break free from the crowd and run out the door and down the steps. Jess is running down the street toward her car as fast as her heels will take her and I sprint to speed up.

I get to her car just as she's turning on the ignition and I throw myself in front of it.

"Jess, stop! Stop!"

There are tears streaming down her face and her makeup is running in black streaks down her cheeks.

"Get out of the way!" She yells. She leans on the horn but I put my hands on the hood of her car. "Move!"

"Jess! It's not what it looks like, I swear!" I hate how pathetic of an excuse that is. I hate seeing her hurt. I hate thinking that I'm the source of those tears. "Jess," I plead.

She honks the horn again until I break and move out of the way. I watch her drive down the street and turn off.

My heart is thumping. My breath is ragged.

"*Fuck*!" I yell, kicking a nearby light pole. Pain explodes in my foot and shoots up through my leg and I wince. I look back at the hotel and see a million curious eyes looking out at me. "What the fuck are you looking at!"

Some of the eyes turn away but most of them keep staring. I turn away and start hopping and limping back to my truck as fast as I can. Every step sends pain through my leg. I've probably broken my fucking toe.

I get in my truck and rev it up, following the path that Jess took to her grandmother's house. I try to slow my breath down and think of what I'll say to her.

I'm desperate. I have to make her understand that I didn't want Mary to kiss me. I didn't even want to be in the office with her in the first place!

My heart sinks when I think about it. I was in the office, and I don't even know if Jess saw me push Mary off me. How can I make her understand that I haven't even looked at another woman since I met her? No one matters except her. No one exists except her!

She's the woman I want. I'm made for her, and she's made for me. She's the mother of my child. I can't let her slip away and I can't ignore what I've been feeling for the past two months.

She's the love of my life.

50

JESS

I THOUGHT my heart was crushed when I found out Owen hadn't told me about his past. I thought I was heartbroken when I didn't speak to him for two months, and I thought it was ripped out of my chest and stomped on when it looked like he didn't want the baby.

It wasn't.

This is what heartbreak feels like.

It's physical, I understand that now. Heartbreak is physical pain. It's an ax splitting my chest in half. It's my stomach squeezing so tight that I feel like I'm going to throw up. It's a throbbing in my temples that feels like my head is going to explode.

My whole body feels as tight as a guitar string, like any movement could snap me in half. I pull the truck in front of Gram's house and kill the engine, still sobbing into the steering wheel.

The house is dark, and I reach into my purse for a tissue. I use the rear-view mirror to wipe my face and clean the streaks of mascara off my cheeks. I take a deep breath and prepare myself to tiptoe upstairs.

I can't let Gram see me like this.

Just as I open the car door and get out, I hear a familiar engine coming down the road. Owen stops his truck with a screech in the middle of the street and jumps out, leaving the engine running and the door wide open.

"Leave me alone," I say. My voice is unsteady and I wish it sounded more forceful.

"Jess, please," Owen says. His eyebrows are knitted together and he takes a step toward me, palms outstretched. "Please just listen to what I have to say."

"Why! Why would I listen to you! One minute you're telling me that you care about me, that you care about the baby and you want to see if we have a future together, and then I turn my back for one minute. I *help my grandmother get into bed* and you've run off with Mary. Fucking. Hanson."

"I didn't run off with anyone, Jess, please. I pushed her off me. The kiss surprised me. I didn't want it!"

"But you did it."

He inhales deeply. It looks like he's about to cry and I look away.

"Jess," he says softly. "I pushed her off. I never kissed her."

I snort. "You know," I start. "The first time I got pregnant by accident, and then the guy I was seeing ran off with Mary, I thought my life was over. This time, I don't know what to think. I think I should laugh but I don't have the energy right now."

"Wait, what? Did... you said he left. He left you for *Mary*? Is that why you hate her so much?"

"Fuck you, Owen." I turn to the house and I hear him come up behind me.

"Jess, please, *please* listen. I pushed her off. I grabbed her face and pushed her backward. I didn't want to be there with her."

I pause and look back at him. "You... grabbed her face?"

He holds up his palm, fingers spread wide, and extends his arms slowly as if he's pushing a door open. I frown slowly as he drops his arm. He chews his lip and shrugs.

"I didn't know what to do," he says. "I panicked."

I stare at him for a few seconds until finally he drops his gaze and kicks my car's tire. Suddenly he's doubled over in pain, grabbing his leg with both hands.

"Fuck!" He yells.

"What!" I say, taking a step toward him. "What's going on? Are you okay?"

"I kicked a fucking light pole when you drove off," he says, wincing as he looks back up at me. "I think I broke my toe."

There's a pause, and then the ridiculousness of the situation starts to get to me. I think about Owen pushing Mary's face away, and the half-embarrassed, half-pained expression on his face as he looks up at me. The laughter starts bubbling up inside me. It starts in my stomach as my shoulders relax down and suddenly, I'm doubled over, leaning on the hood of my car as the peals of laughter spill out of me. Owen sits on the car and laughs, looking over at me and shaking his head.

"You are an idiot," I say when I can finally speak again.

"I know," he responds. He sighs and then looks at me with eyes wide. "Come on, Jess, you're the one that I want. You and that baby," he says, looking down at my stomach.

I smile and slide in beside him. "How's the toe," I ask gently, resting my head on his shoulder.

He snorts. "It hurts. Like, a lot."

"I bet. Come on, get in here. Let me get you some ice," I say, hopping past him to turn off his truck, close the door and then extend my hand toward him.

The instant my arm is wrapped around his waist my whole body feels like it's melting. All the tension that has gripped me ever since I found out I was pregnant disappears. He puts his arm around my shoulder and we slowly limp up the pathway to the house.

"So when you say grabbed her by the face..." I say as I open the front door.

Owen chuckles softly and shakes his head. "Whoever said chivalry was dead was out of their mind."

I laugh and squeeze my arm around his waist a bit tighter. "Come on, let's go to the kitchen. I'll get you some ice."

51

OWEN

I DON'T EVEN FEEL my toe anymore. All I feel is Jess's body next to mine and her arm wrapped around my waist as she helps me into a chair at the kitchen table. She pulls up another chair beside me and speaks quietly.

"Get your leg up," she says, motioning to the chair. "I'll get some ice."

I watch her work as she pulls the freezer door open. "Ah!" She says as she takes out a bag of frozen peas and holds them up triumphantly. "Perfect."

She slips my shoe off and slowly peels off my sock. I wince. My foot is already black and blue, and my big toe is incredibly swollen. Jess whistles.

"Ouch," she says and I groan. "You should go to the hospital tomorrow morning."

"Sounds like torture," I say, thinking of long hours in a hospital waiting room. "What would they even do? They wouldn't give me a cast, would they? Don't toes just heal on their own?"

"They'd take an x-ray and make sure it was broken," she says as she puts the peas under my foot and starts wrapping a bandage around it. "I don't know, I'm not a doctor. They'd give you crutches, probably."

Once the foot is wrapped, I sit back and close my eyes. The frozen peas are helping to dull the ache. Jess moves behind me and slides her hands onto my shoulders. I groan as she starts massaging them slowly, working her way across my shoulders and up into my scalp.

"That's so nice," I say in a low voice. My cock starts to pulse, even with her just touching my shoulders. She's close enough that I can smell her perfume and I can feel the heat of her body near my head. I groan again.

She rubs my shoulders softly for a second and then gives me a light squeeze. "Come on," she says. "Let's get you home. I'll drive your truck back."

Her words surprise me but I nod quickly. Of course she'd want me to leave. What did I think was going to happen at her grandmother's place? I swing my leg off the chair and she helps me to my feet. The bag of peas is firmly strapped to the bottom of my foot. She slips a pair of flip-flops on as we walk out the front door and I hop on one foot beside her. I try not to put too much weight down on her slight body but she squeezes me close and supports me as I walk.

"Up you go," she says with a groan as she helps me into the passenger's seat. I watch her walk around the front of the truck and lift herself up into the driver's seat. She slams the door closed and looks at me with a grin. "Who's the knight in shining armor now?"

I laugh. "The tables have turned."

The truck revs to life and we start driving slowly. It's a short drive back to the hotel, and I can hear the music from the wedding still blaring down the street. She pulls the truck over in front of the hotel and jogs around to my side to help me down. I can already see the eyes starting to appear at the hotel entrance.

Jess glances over at the people staring at us and chuckles. "They don't miss anything, do they."

We do our walk-hop up the steps and over to the lobby. I sigh as I put my hand on the bannister, resting for a moment before the long climb up the stairs. My foot is throbbing. Jess puts a hand on my back.

"Come on," she says gently. "You can do it."

One step at a time, I hop all the way up to the top landing. When we're at the top, Jess guides me to my door. I fumble with my keys and she clears her throat.

"I'm going to head back," she says.

My eyebrows shoot up as I glance up at her. She's chewing her lip and staring off down the hallway to the stairs. I clear my throat and nod quickly.

"Yeah, of course. Sure. Thank you," I say. "For everything."

"Call me tomorrow? We can grab a bite to eat, I think we have a lot to talk about."

"Definitely."

There's a pause as the two of us stare at each other. Finally, I can't take it anymore. I slide my fingers over her jaw and pull her into me. My lips crush against hers and my heart explodes in my chest. She wraps her arms against me and once again I feel like I'm exactly where I'm meant to be. I kiss her over and over, tasting those lips that I've missed so much. I wrap my other arm around her waist and feel her body pressed up against mine. I never want this to end.

We finally separate and I rest my forehead against hers. We just stand there holding each other for a few breaths.

"Call me tomorrow," she says gently as she lifts her eyes up to mine. She smiles tentatively and strokes my cheek. "I need to go home."

"You sure you don't want to come in?" I ask, already knowing the answer.

"I need some time to think, Owen. I'm exhausted. I'll see you tomorrow, I promise."

I nod. "Of course. I'll see you tomorrow."

"Take my truck," I say, pushing my keys toward her. "It's too late to walk."

She shakes her head gently. "I need the fresh air. Thanks though."

Jess smiles gently and I lay one last kiss on her lips. She slips out of my arms and squeezes my hand as she turns away. I watch her walk down the hall in her long dress and old flip-flops until she disappears down the stairs.

With a huge sigh, I turn to my door and slide the key in the lock. I swing it open and step through, closing it behind me as I rub my forehead. I almost jump out of my skin when a voice speaks from the darkness.

"Hello, Owen," it says.

I look up and my chest feels hollow. The blood drains from my face and I feel my Adam's apple bob up and down as I swallow.

"Dad," I say. "What are you doing here?"

52

JESS

I walk away slowly, down the street toward Gram's house. My mind is turbulent and I'm not sure what to think. I'm not sure if being on my own tonight is the right thing to do. Everything in my body was screaming at me to stay beside him, to curl up on his bed and wrap my arms around him, but I just can't.

I need to think about this. Everything is too rushed, too intense, too quick. I don't even know what I want. I went from thinking he was sleeping with Mary to thinking he's devoted to me in about an hour. Before that, I went from thinking he wanted nothing to do with the baby to believing him when he said he wanted to be with me. My head is completely melted.

I know I want to be with him. Gram was right: some things are worth pursuing. I've gone through a roller coaster of emotions today, and all I know for sure is that when I'm with him I'm happy.

Before I know it, I'm walking up the big flagstones to Gram's front porch. I open the door gently and slip inside, trying not to let the stairs creak as I make my way up to my room. I open the door and sigh. Even though I'm almost thirty years old, this bedroom still feels like home.

Suddenly I'm exhausted. My bones ache and every muscle in my body is screaming. I unzip my bridesmaid's dress and let it puddle at my feet and then take out the ten thousand pins in my hair before climbing into bed. I don't have the energy to take my makeup off or put my clothes away or brush my teeth. Within seconds, I'm asleep.

I WAKE up and groan as the sunlight hits my face. I forgot to close my curtains last night. I roll over and check the time, and then strain my ears to hear if Gram is awake and buzzing downstairs. I frown when all I hear is complete silence. Usually she would be up by now, but maybe she was extra tired after the wedding yesterday.

I check the time again. It's almost 8 a.m. I rub my eyes and groan when I see the black makeup streaked on my knuckles where I rubbed. I probably look like a raccoon now. I wrap a towel around myself and head to the bathroom.

I almost burst out laughing when I see myself in the mirror. My hair, which was so carefully hair-sprayed last night is sticking up in all directions. I look like Medusa. My makeup is streaked and blotchy, with big dark patches under my eyes. I'm definitely not as glamorous as I was last night.

The shower is hot and I take my time. I wash my hair slowly, massaging my scalp. I wash my face and body thoroughly and then just stand under the hot water without moving.

My thoughts drift to Owen and a smile forms on my lips. He cares about me. I can feel it in every touch and I can see it in his eyes. My heart starts beating a bit harder when I say it to myself again: he cares about me, and he cares about this baby.

All this drama, all the back and forth and hot and cold isn't right. We should just be open with each other and talk about these things like adults. I need to settle down and stop being so afraid that he'll leave me. I need to listen to Gram, and allow myself to open up. If I stop freaking out and running away every time I think he'll hurt me, I'd let myself just be with him. I'd let myself be loved.

I take a deep breath and turn off the shower. Today, I'll lay it all out for him. I'll tell him that I'm willing to give it a shot with us, but we have to be completely honest with each other. I don't want to live in this town, and I don't want to raise my kid somewhere where I've always felt like an outsider. I want to know that he'll be there for me and for the kid, and that he has to tell me everything about his past and his plans for the future.

I can tell him all this and then I can tell him that being with him makes me feel better than anything else I've ever felt. It excites me to my core.

I finally step out of the shower and dry myself off. When I look in the mirror, I look like myself again. I smile as I put moisturizer on and start my morning routine. There's a lightness in my movements and even though I'm nervous about talking to Owen, I know what I want now and I'm not afraid to say it to him.

I can be an adult about this.

I hum to myself as I get dressed and head downstairs. I glance in the kitchen and frown. Everything is exactly how I left it last night, which means Gram hasn't been up yet. I turn on the coffee and make myself some toast while it brews.

I pour out two mugs of coffee and leave one of them next to my toast. I smile as I make my way up the stairs and over to Gram's bedroom. My knuckles tap softly on the door while I call out to her.

"Gram? Are you up? I've got some coffee for you!"

I wait a few seconds and lean my ear to the door. Silence.

I knock again, a bit louder this time. "Gram! Are you there?"

Complete silence. There's not a noise on the other side of the door, no rustling or sighing or grunt to answer my knocks. I frown as my hand hovers over the doorknob. With a deep breath, I turn it and push the door open.

Gram is still in bed, exactly how I left her last night. I walk over and speak softly to her. "Gram? I think you should get up. You'll miss the day!"

She stays completely still. It starts to dawn on me that something is wrong. Her eyes are closed and she's sleeping peacefully, arms over her heart. I get closer and it seems too still, too peaceful. My hands start to shake and the coffee begins to slosh around in the mug.

It's not until I get right next to the bed that I know she's gone. The coffee mug drops out of my hand and shatters on the wooden floorboards, sending coffee all over the floor. I ignore it, eyes glued on Gram. My voice is trembling.

"Gram?"

Finally, I touch her skin and shiver. It's ice cold. My chest feels like the weight of the earth is pressed on it and I sit down on the bed beside her, grabbing both her shoulders and shaking her.

"Gram! Gram! Wake up! Wake up!" My voice starts to crack. The pain in my chest radiates out to the rest of my body as I collapse on top of her and sob. The lightness in my heart from this morning is replaced with sharp, searing pain as I rest my head against my grandmother's chest. My tears seep into her nightgown and I tremble as I realize that I'll never hear her voice again.

    She's gone.

53

OWEN

I WAKE up as the sun comes up, so I guess I slept a bit last night. It's surprising, considering the visitor I had in my room when I got in. I groan and roll onto my side. The mushy bag of thawed peas slides to the floor and I move my feet off the big wet patch the peas left. My foot is throbbing and I glance down to see it just as swollen as it was yesterday. I sigh and lie back down.

My father's words are still ringing in my ears. When I saw him last night, my heart almost stopped. He grinned at me like the Cheshire Cat sitting alone in the darkness.

"Owen, my son," he growled from his perch on my bed. I'd stayed completely still, afraid to move in case he pounced. "I haven't seen or heard from you in months."

"I've been busy," I responded, scanning the room for someone else.

"Calm down," he said, "I'm alone."

"I thought you weren't allowed to leave the state during the trial?"

My father chuckled. "And yet here we are." His eyes narrowed and a grin spread across his lips. In the darkness it looked more like a snarl. "Now. Your mother tells me that you don't want to be part of the family business."

"I've never wanted to be part of the family business," I'd spat at him. I stumbled over to my dresser and leaned against it to relieve the pressure in my foot.

"What happened to you?"

"Nothing. What do you want?"

"I want you to understand that if you don't let me use this nice little hotel as a new flagship for the business, I'm going to get angry. And you know what happens when I get angry."

His eyes had narrowed and a chill went down my spine.

"You want to use the hotel— the business that I've built myself—for your own fucking fraud? No! Absolutely not! Get out."

My father had rolled his eyes and leaned back in my bed. He looked at me with one eyebrow raised and shook his head. "Wrong choice."

"What are you going to do?"

"Well, I was going to use that little money-hungry whore to blackmail you with a sexual harassment lawsuit, but the bitch couldn't even do that right. So now we're onto plan B."

I frowned as I tried to make sense of his words. "Mary? You put Mary up to this?"

He just sighed and waved his hand lazily. "She was useful for one thing," he'd added as his eyes swung back to mine. I'd gripped the dresser harder as his gaze almost knocked me back. Pure, black fury stared back at me. "She did tell me some interesting information about your new girlfriend."

"Don't you fucking—"

My father had laughed and finally lifted himself off the bed. "Don't worry. I'm not going to hurt her. That is, I'm not going to hurt her if you don't cause any trouble. That's plan C."

"Fuck you," I'd spat at him. He'd shrugged and straightened his jacket before walking past me toward the door.

"Your funeral," he'd said as he opened it and stepped through.

Now, even though he's been gone from my room for hours, I can still smell his cologne in my sheets. I can still taste the bitterness of his anger in my mouth and all I want to do is scream.

My own father tried to blackmail me. I wonder how much he paid Mary to come onto me. I wonder what he's done to her now that it hasn't worked. I wonder what he has planned, and why he mentioned Jess.

I sigh and rub my eyes with my palms. Something ignites in me when I think of Jess and our unborn child. I can't let him hurt her. I won't let him hurt her! I sit up as my heart starts beating faster. I need to stop him. Any loyalty that I had toward him—any residual filial love—is gone. He's not my father. He's nothing to me, and now he's threatening to destroy the one thing I care about.

Pain shoots through my foot as I hobble over to the dresser. Gingerly, I try to put weight on my foot and stumble as the pain blinds me.

Wincing, I grunt as I lean against the dresser. I won't be able to do much to stop him if I can't walk.

I pull open the bottom drawer of my dresser and frown as I see my clothes in a mess. My heart starts beating as I reach over to the spot with the files. My jaw drops and I push the clothes to the other side, and finally rip every item of clothing out of the drawer.

"No, no, no, no!" I yell as I see everything is gone. I sit down on the floor and hold my head in my hands, rocking back and forth.

He must have taken them. He knows that I had them.

That must be why he made the trip himself. Now he's here, he knows I had incriminating files against him, and he knows that Jess means a lot to me. Any protection that I had for being his son, any leverage that I could have used to keep him friendly is *gone*.

I glance over at my bedside table and see my keys. The USB is hanging off my key chain, a little black rectangle staring back at me. I lift myself up and take the keys in my hand, flicking the USB open and closed a couple times.

He may know that I had enough evidence to send him to jail, but now he thinks he's got it. If I act quickly, I still have the upper hand.

54

JESS

When my tears dry, I lift myself off Gram's chest. I stroke her cheek gently and sigh. My eyes sweep around the room, taking in the spilled coffee, the bright sunlight, the perfectly tidy closet.

What do you even do when someone dies? I stand up and pick up the mug off the floor, staring into it for answers. Do I call 9-1-1? It's not like there's anything they could do.

Not knowing what else to do, I dial the number.

"9-1-1, what's your emergency?"

"Uh, not so much an emergency," my voice catches in my throat and I take a deep breath. "My grandmother died in the night. I found her this morning and I don't know what to do." On the last word, my voice breaks and I hear the dispatcher's voice soften.

"Okay, dear. No problem. Do you know what happened? Was it an accident?"

"She's eighty-two years old. She just went to bed, and—" My voice breaks again.

"I'm going to send police and an ambulance and they'll be

able to assess the situation and help you out, okay? Can you give me your address?"

Somehow, I make it through the phone call without bursting into tears. In a daze I walk downstairs to wait for the police and paramedics. I open the front door and sit down on the front steps, staring at the quiet street but seeing nothing.

Suddenly the past few days make sense. Gram telling me she loved me, telling me to find happiness, telling me not to waste any time. She knew she was dying.

"Why didn't you say anything," I whisper to myself as a tear spills over onto my cheek. I brush it away quickly and take a deep breath.

I know why she didn't say anything, it's because she didn't want to be a burden. She just wanted to live her life quietly, and die quietly in her own house. Now the tears are coming faster and I can't keep up with brushing them away. I take a deep breath and try to pull myself together when I see the emergency vehicles turn down the street.

The rest of the morning is a blur. There's lots of questions, lots of kind words, lots of phone calls. Finally a man in a black suit from a funeral home comes and collects her, and I watch as he drives away with my grandmother's body.

The last of the emergency vehicles leaves and I'm alone. I'm completely alone and I'm empty. I walk from room to room like a zombie.

After who knows how long, I hear a truck outside the house. I walk out the front door to see Owen sliding down from the driver's seat. He's still hobbling, and obviously hasn't been to the doctor. He looks like he hasn't slept all night.

"Jess, you're okay!"

"Yeah," I answer. "I guess."

Owen frowns and hobbles toward me a little bit faster. I

come down the steps and give him my arm to steady him. He takes it and stares at my face.

"What's wrong?"

A lump forms in my throat and my eyes start to water. I open and close my mouth like a goldfish and Owen slides his arm around me.

"What's wrong, Jess?" He asks again. His voice sounds panicked. "What happened?"

"Gram died," I finally answer. "They just took the body away."

Owen stares at me, wide-eyed, before letting all the air out of his lungs. He hops up to face me and wraps his arms around me. I melt into him, and for the first time since I found Gram, I let it all go. The tears come fast and heavy and pretty soon his tee-shirt is soaked. He just stands there and holds me as I cry.

We sway to one side and I hear him make a muffled sound. I pull away.

"Sorry!" I say. "I forgot about your foot. Why haven't you been to the doctor? Come on, let's go inside."

He takes my hand and hops up toward the front door. With some shuffling and hopping, he's through the door and settled on the couch in the living room. I go to the kitchen and come back with two cups of coffee. I sit down beside him and fold my foot under my body as he drapes his arm over my shoulder. My head fits perfectly onto his chest and I sigh.

"We really should be getting you to a doctor but it just feels too good to be here like this," I whisper.

"Shh," he says, stroking my arm. He turns toward me and kisses the top of my head. "I'm just glad you're not hurt."

"Why would I be hurt?"

"I was just worried when you didn't answer my calls, that's all."

"Did you call?" I shift my weight and pull out my phone. Sure enough, four missed calls and three messages, all from Owen. "Oh."

He chuckles, and then takes a deep breath. "Jess, I need to ask you a favor, and I know it's awful timing but it's really important."

I lift my head and search his face. "What are you talking about?"

"It's a long story," he says. I raise an eyebrow and he sighs again. "How good is your grandmother's internet?"

55

OWEN

Jess laughs and rolls her eyes. "What are you talking about?"

I want to tell her everything, from beginning to end, but I don't know where to start. She's staring at me, lifting herself off me and frowning. I put my hand on her thigh.

"I had a visit from my dad last night," I finally say. "He was paying Mary to try to blackmail me with a sexual harassment lawsuit. He knows about you."

Jess leans away a bit further. Her brows knit together and she shakes her head. "What? What are you talking about? Owen. What the fuck are you talking about? I'm not in the mood for this bullshit. In case you forgot, my one remaining family member died a couple hours ago."

Her words bite through me and I squeeze her thigh gently with my hand. "I know. I know! Look," I take a deep breath. "My parents have been trying to use me to continue syphoning money for themselves. They want to use the hotel. I refused, obviously, and this was my dad's idea of a threat."

"A threat? You told me you had nothing to do with the trial!"

"I didn't! I don't! I didn't know it was going on until after the case against me was thrown out. I found some old files in the office that proved my dad was guilty."

"Did you hand them to the police?" She's staring at me, wide-eyed.

"No," I say, sighing. My face contorts into a grimace and I put my hand on my forehead. "I wanted to, but I couldn't bring myself to betray my family like that. I kept telling myself that they loved me, that they'd kept me separate from it all to protect me. That's why I didn't tell you about any of it when we first met. I just couldn't lie to you and tell you they were innocent, and I couldn't betray them by telling someone they were guilty."

She stays quiet, her face stone still. I take a deep breath and continue.

"Jess, believe me, I wanted to tell you. From the moment I met you I've wanted to tell you everything about me. It's not until I saw my dad last night that I realized they weren't protecting me, and they don't care about me. They were just keeping me clean in case they needed to use my name when they got caught." I sigh, and lift my eyes up to her. "He threatened me. He threatened you! And fuck! I'm not going to let anything happen to you."

Jess is completely still. She hasn't moved at all and I can't tell what she's thinking.

"I fucking love you, Jess. My dad took the files last night but I have a copy." I hold up my keys, showing her the USB. "I need you to send these files to this email," I say, giving her the piece of paper with the prosecutor's email on it. "And then I need you to disappear. Just go away from here, go back to New York. I don't know if they're following me or if they're following you, but you just need to get as far away from me as possible."

Finally, Jess moves. She shakes her head from side to side and starts to cry.

"No," she says. "No, no!" She takes a deep, trembling breath and puts her hand on my chest. "I just lost my grandmother. You're the father of my child and you're all I have left. I'm not leaving. I'll take you to the hospital and send the files from there. You'll be safe there. They won't be able to do anything. I am not leaving."

Her bottom lip trembles and I wrap my arms around her. She's shaking, and I just stroke her gently. I shouldn't be burdening her with this, I should just be comforting her after her grandmother's death! I'm thrusting all my problems onto her at the very moment when she probably needs my support. I chew on her words and nod slowly. "Okay. Let's stay together, Jess. I don't want to let you out of my sight. Not today, not ever again. You're stuck with me now."

I feel Jess let out a small laugh as she rests against my chest. She nods.

"Let me drop the truck back at the hotel so it looks like I'm still around," I say. "And then we can go to the hospital and get this toe checked out."

Jess nods, and then grins. "With any luck, you'll be stuck in the waiting room for hours."

I laugh and nod. "If I'm lucky."

She takes the email and USB from me and tucks them into her purse along with her laptop. She stands up straighter and nods to me before swinging her eyes around the room and sighing. I groan as I stand up and put my hands around her waist.

"Thank you," I say. "I know today is probably the worst day of your life. You're the strongest woman I've ever met."

She shakes her head. "It's not the worst day of my life. We're together, so it can't be the worst day of my life."

My heart grows in my chest and I take a deep breath. Jess wraps her arms around me and we hold each other for a few moments. Her voice is muffled against my chest when she speaks again.

"Did you mean it?"

"Mean what?"

"Did you mean it when you said you fucking love me?" She moves her head to look at me and grins. "Is that the old romantic coming out of you again?"

"I love the shit out of you," I respond with a grin. She laughs and rolls her eyes. I take a deep breath and say it again: "I love you, Jess. With all my heart."

Her eyes start to mist and she takes a deep breath. "I think I love you too." Her voice is barely above a whisper but it sounds as loud as a roar to my ears. My chest bursts and I hold her tighter against me, drinking in every second we have together. Our lips meet and once again I feel like I'm whole again. I could kiss this woman for the rest of time.

Finally, she pulls away and strokes my cheek. "Let's go."

I nod. "Yeah. Let's go."

56

JESS

My heart is thumping as we drive out of Lexington. It's a twenty minute drive to the nearest hospital, and my hands are gripping the steering wheel so hard my knuckles are turning white. Owen reaches over and slides a hand over my thigh. The warmth is comforting and I finally feel my shoulders relax.

"It'll be okay," Owen says. I glance over at him and try to smile. He smiles and nods. "I promise."

"It's just been a rough day," I answer. His hand squeezes my thigh gently and he sighs.

"I can't tell you how much I appreciate this. Your grandmother was one of the kindest people I've ever met, and this town definitely won't be the same without her."

My throat tightens and I nod, blinking away the tears. "There's nothing there for me now. Don't make me cry," I say with a bitter laugh. "I might crash the car."

He squeezes my leg again. "I meant what I said last night, Jess. I'm here for you. I love you, and I want to be there for you and the baby."

I nod my head, hoping that's enough because I don't trust

my voice. He strokes my thigh gently as I check my rear-view mirror. I just want to get to the hospital already.

Owen takes his hand off my thigh and pulls out his phone. The space on my leg where his hand used to be feels strangely empty, and I glance over to see him dialing a number. He puts the cell phone to his ear and I glance over, waiting to hear him speak.

"Mr. Vanier," he says after a few seconds. "It's Owen McAllister." He nods a couple times as he listens, and then speaks again. "I've come across some files that could be of interest for your investigation. I'm ready to make a deal."

My heart starts beating faster and I glance over at Owen again. He must be talking to the prosecutor in his father's case. His eyes are glued on the road and I can't tell what he's thinking. He shakes his head, as if the man on the other end of the line could see him.

"These files will be very, *very* helpful to you. I don't have much time. Send through the paperwork and I'll sign it. I want complete immunity for myself and a guarantee that my assets won't be frozen along with my father's company." There's another pause as he listens and he sighs in frustration. "No. Those are my terms." He glances over at me and then nods again. "Thanks. I'll wait for your email."

He hangs up the phone and takes a deep breath. His hand slides back onto my thigh and I try to relax into my seat and ignore the thumping of my heart. The drive seems longer than usual, but finally we pull into the hospital parking lot.

"Wait here," I say, jogging to the entrance. I grab a wheelchair and come back to the car. Owen is leaning against the passenger's side door and sighs with relief.

"I'm seriously sick of hopping on one foot," he says with a grin.

I laugh. "I figured. Now let's just hope that you're here for a nice long wait."

I grab my purse out of the car and lock everything up before getting behind Owen and wheeling him to the hospital entrance. As soon as we move inside the sliding glass doors, I breathe a sigh of relief. Soon, we're talking to the triage nurse and being directed to a waiting room. I settle into a chair beside Owen and pull out my laptop.

"Okay, do you want to send these files from my email or yours?"

"Mine would probably be best," Owen says. "I'll wait for Vanier's deal before sending anything."

I nod and fire up my laptop, taking out my phone to get the hotspot working and angling the screen toward him. "You can log into your email, and then I guess we just wait. I'll get the files ready to send."

Owen taps away and logs into his email. He hands the computer back to me and I glance at his inbox.

"Nothing yet?" I ask. He shakes his head.

"Not yet."

I slide the USB into the port at the side of the computer and wait for it to load. As soon as my computer reads it, Owen points to a file on the screen.

Movies

I raise an eyebrow. "Movies?"

He laughs. "I was trying to think of a file name that would be the most inconspicuous. You know, hide things in plain sight."

"Smart," I say, moving the mouse over the file. I click on it to open and a box pops up on the screen. I frown. "Password protected?"

Owen's brow knits together. "I forgot about that." I turn the computer to face him and his hands hover over the keyboard. He chews his lip and then glances at me.

I shake my head. "You're joking."

He cringes and looks back at the screen. My mouth drops and I shake my head again.

"You don't remember?"

"I remember, I just don't know what it is," he says. I frown and he glances at me again. "I used my truck's registration number. It was sitting on my desk when I copied the files, so I figured I'd have access to it and it would be hard to hack."

I can't help it—I start laughing in disbelief. After this morning with Gram, and then the stress of the drive and getting Owen to the hospital, and now this? He can't remember his freaking password? My laugh starts as a soft chuckle and pretty soon my hand is smacked against my forehead and I'm doubled over. I glance over at Owen who looks embarrassed as he starts to laugh with me.

"Hack? What do you think this is, a sci-fi movie?"

Owen shakes his head, laughs and then shrugs. "I don't know. I was trying to be careful."

"We are the worst secret agents ever. So where's your registration?" I ask, knowing the answer.

"It's in my truck."

"The truck that we left at the hotel to throw people off our trail?" I ask as another bitter laugh slips through my lips.

"Yeah," he says. "That truck."

57

OWEN

I watch Jess walk back out the sliding glass doors and I'm kicking myself. I hate thinking of her going back to the Lex and I hate thinking of her being alone.

I can't believe I did that. I can't believe I forgot the fact that I'd protected it with a password. I outsmarted myself.

That's what I'll tell myself, anyways.

The waiting room is relatively empty, but by the looks of the other patients, my broken toe will be way down the list. There's a couple young kids and a man that looks like he's about to pass out. I should be here for a few hours at least.

I refresh the computer and sigh. Still nothing from Vanier.

My ringtone almost makes me jump out of my skin. One of the kid's mothers looks over at me and frowns as I fumble to get my phone out. I don't recognize the number and I hesitate for a second before pressing 'answer'.

"Hello?"

"Owen, my dear son," my dad croons over the phone. "How are you today? Did you have time to think about our little chat?"

"I had time to think that you could go fuck yourself," I say a little too loud. The mother looks at me again in horror, turning her child away from me and glancing over her shoulder. I slump in my chair and huddle the phone to my ear.

"I thought you might say that," he replies. "I found your little stash of files. Looks like you haven't been the loyal son I thought you were."

Even after everything, even though I know he's been threatening me and threatening Jess, his words still hurt. I've always been loyal, up until he tried to use me as his scapegoat.

"I know. You've got them now, so I'm basically fucked, aren't I?" I ignore the mother's huff behind me. I really shouldn't swear this much.

"Basically, yeah," my dad replies. "So are you going to agree to transfer your hotel over to the company?"

"No. I'm not going to let you do this."

"Well, looks like you've chosen Plan B. Is that your final answer?"

"Fuck you," I spit.

My father chuckles and then sighs. The last thing I hear is a click as the line goes dead. I blow out all the air from my lungs and lean my head back against the hard plastic seat, rubbing my eyes with the fingers of one hand. I lift my phone up and hesitate, my finger hovering over the number he just called from.

I shouldn't have done that.

Now he's mad, and he knows I won't cooperate. Jess is out there, driving as fast as she can back toward the hotel—back to him.

Why did I do that? I let my anger get in the way and now once again, I've put Jess in the crosshairs.

"Fuck," I say under my breath. The mother makes a noise

and stands up, herding her child to the other end of the waiting room. I sigh. I don't have the energy for this right now.

I flick through my phone and dial Jess's number.

"Come on, come on, come on," I say. Even if I can't keep my father on my side, the least I can do is warn her about what just happened and tell her to be careful.

My heart sinks when I hear a phone ringing beside me and I look down to see Jess's purse. She must have just grabbed my truck's keys and her own car keys and headed out the door. I hang up and her phone stops ringing.

I let out a big sigh and lean my head back in the chair. We definitely are the worst secret agents ever. The criminals from 'Home Alone' would be better than we are at doing this.

I rub my forehead one more time and try to get comfortable in the tiny, hard chairs. I glance around the waiting room again and see the mother in the corner, scowling at me. There's one more enemy for my growing list.

I close my eyes and lean back. All I can do now is wait. Wait for Jess, wait for the email from Vanier, wait for the doctor. Just wait and hope.

58

JESS

THE UNCONTROLLABLE LAUGHTER that overcame me in the waiting room is long since gone. I stare at the straight road, glancing periodically in my rear view mirror. Shaking my head, I try to take a deep breath to calm my nerves. Even if someone was following me, what would I do? How would I even know?

I need to calm down.

I flick on the radio and switch from station to station until I finally turn it off. Silence is better. The road stretches on and on and on until I worry that I've taken a wrong turn. It didn't seem this long on the way here.

Finally, signs for Lexington start appearing. My heart starts thumping in my chest as I drive the last few miles into my small hometown, slowing down as I turn onto Main Street.

Everything seems normal and it's almost eerie. I park my car a block away from the Lex and jump out, closing and locking the doors and shuffling away.

"Jess!" Someone calls out behind me. I turn to see Sam jogging toward me. She has concern all over her face and she wraps me in a hug. "I'm so sorry, Jess. I'm so sorry about your grandma. I just heard. I tried calling you!"

"I haven't really been looking at my phone," I say, glancing over to the hotel looming behind me. Sam puts her hands on my arms and squeezes.

"Are you okay? You look like hell."

I take a deep breath. Even if I had time to talk to her, the last thing I want to think about is Gram. Anytime the hint of her creeps into my mind, my whole body goes tense and my eyes start prickling. Right now, being the worst secret agent in the world is a lot better than being a grieving granddaughter. Anything is better than that.

"I'm okay," I finally respond. I take a deep breath. "I'm okay. Don't worry about me. You should be enjoying married life! Aren't you supposed to leave on your honeymoon soon?"

"We were supposed to head out this morning but I didn't want to leave without seeing you."

My heart breaks and I finally look Sam in the eye. She has so much love and concern for me and I almost fall over. The walls that I've built up today to avoid the reality of Gram's death start to crack and I shake my head.

"You shouldn't have done that. You'll miss your flight!"

"We have time, and there are lots of flights. Come on, why don't you come back to my mom's place."

"You would skip your honeymoon for me?" I ask, my voice breaking.

Sam grins. "Well, delay. Let's not get carried away here."

I try to laugh but it comes out as a gurgle. I wrap my arms around her and she hugs me tightly. In that moment, I realize that I'm not alone. I'm not alone at all! This morning when Gram died, I felt like I'd lost everything, but here I am with a man who loves me and wants to be with me and our child, and a friend who delayed her honeymoon to make sure I'm okay.

My eyes are watering and I pull away. "Go, Sam. I'm okay. Really. I would feel worse if you missed your flight for me."

Sam stares at me for a few moments. I watch her swallow and then nod slowly. "Okay. I'll call you tonight. I love you."

"I love you too," I answer. "I'm sorry I left your wedding early and caused a scene."

Sam laughs. "It wouldn't be a real wedding without some drama, right? Are you okay?"

"I'm good," I nod. "I think Owen and I are... going out." In love? Together? I don't know how grown-ups talk about relationships. Sam just laughs and gives me one more hug. My heart feels a tiny bit lighter. When I say goodbye, I watch her walk away and I feel like part of her is still with me, right beside Owen in my heart. I'm not alone at all.

With renewed courage I turn to the Lex. I take a deep breath and start shuffling toward the building, turning the corner and slipping to the back where the truck is parked. In a few minutes this whole thing should be close to being over.

When I get to the truck, my hands shake as I try to unlock the passenger's side door. Finally, the key slides in and the lock pops open. I open the door and pull the glove compartment open.

Papers fall out all over the place.

"For fuck's sake," I breathe, trying to gather the sheets of paper before they fall out of the car. I look at each of them in turn, trying to find Owen's registration.

I've looked at a dozen papers when I see some movement in the corner of my eye. I glance up to see someone shuffling toward the back of the Lex, carrying something heavy.

I crouch down and glance up again, frowning. I can't tell

who it is, they've got a hoodie up and a cap on. From their size, I would guess it's a woman.

My eyes flick to Owen's dash camera. *Knight in shining armor after all,* I think. Slowly, I move my hand to press the button. The little red light comes on and the camera starts recording. I just hope it's good enough to catch what's going on.

I watch the figure move toward the building, struggling with a big box or suitcase by their side. With horror, I watch as the suitcase is overturned and liquid starts pouring out.

It's not a suitcase, it's a jerry can, and that's gasoline.

"Hey!" I yell. "Hey! Stop!"

The person glances at me and shakes the can more vigorously. I start running toward them when they finally lift their head. I almost skid to a stop as my jaw drops to the floor.

"Mary?"

59

OWEN

If there was an award for watching a doorway, I would win it. My eyes haven't left those sliding glass doors since I watched Jess walk out of them. I glance at the time—she should be at the Lex by now, if she's not driving back already.

If only she had her phone and I could make sure she was okay! This is killing me. I refresh the computer one more time and finally see a new email come in. My heart starts thumping as I open it up and scan the contents.

It's exactly what I was waiting for: immunity in exchange for the documents. I open it up and start reading more closely when I hear my name called.

"Owen McAllister? Owen *McAllister*?"

There's a woman wearing scrubs and a low ponytail sweeping her eyes around the room. I cough and stand up, holding the laptop as I shuffle to my feet.

"Yep! Here!" She motions me to sit back down in the wheelchair.

"Hi Owen, we're going to get you some x-rays. Can you come this way?"

"Yeah, one second," I say, closing the laptop and trying to gather my things and Jess's. "That was quick!"

"Pretty quiet today," the nurse responds. She gets behind the wheelchair and starts pushing me. I grip the bag and laptop to my chest as we move down the hallways.

"How long is this going to take?" I ask, looking down at the laptop and then glancing back over my shoulder at the door. "My girlfriend will be back soon. I don't want her to worry."

"It'll be a few minutes. Don't worry, you'll be back out there in no time."

I nod, and grip the laptop a bit closer to my chest. We twist and turn down stark white hallways until I see signs pointing to X-RAY. The nurse wheels me into a room and points to a hospital gown.

"Leave your things here. Get that gown on and then come out here to the x-ray."

With that, she closes a curtain and I'm left to get undressed. I sigh, putting the purse and laptop down in the corner of the change room. I hate leaving it there, hate leaving the USB unattended, hate not knowing where Jess is and when she'll be back, but there's nothing I can do.

I change and hop out to the main room. The x-ray technician guides me to the big table and places a heavy lead vest over my shoulders. She positions me on the table and I wince as she moves my foot back and forth, periodically going behind a wall to take the x-rays.

It doesn't take long before I'm back in my clothes and being wheeled back into the waiting room.

"Doesn't look like she's back yet," the nurse says with a smile. "Told you we'd be quick!"

"Thanks," I respond, trying to sound sincere. I glance at

the door and take a deep breath. She should be here by now. She should definitely be here by now. I hug the laptop to my chest and feel for the USB.

Everything is here, I'm just back to waiting and staring at that sliding glass door.

60

JESS

"What are you doing! Mary! Stop!" I yell, sprinting toward her.

"Don't move!" She shouts back, holding her hand up. She drops the gas can and flicks a lighter with one hand, holding her other hand up for me to stop. I skid to a stop and stare at her, my chest heaving up and down as I pant.

"What are you doing? Mary, stop! This is insane!"

Mary's bottom lip is shaking. "Don't move," she repeats, but this time her voice starts to crack. "I'll do it!"

"Why?" I ask. "Put the lighter down."

I try to take a step toward her but she brandishes the lighter at me and her bottom lip shakes some more. Tears start streaming down her face and I glance down at the jerry can, tipped over at her feet. Gas is still glugging out of it and seeping into the ground. I look up at the old timber building and shudder. If she drops that lighter, the whole thing will be gone within minutes.

"What's going on, Mary?"

"You had to come back! You had to come back and fuck everything up again! Why couldn't you just stay away!"

She's crying now, her whole body is shaking.

"What do you mean? What did I fuck up?" I have no idea what she's talking about.

"Why does everyone love you so much? You're always the fucking favorite and what am I? I'm always second best. You're the daughter of a WHORE and everyone loves you! Why!" She moves the lighter closer to the ground and I try to take a step closer to her. She makes a noise and I stop.

"Is that what this is about?" I ask gently. "Are you... are you jealous of me?" She sniffles and I frown. "Why?"

It's a genuine question. I look at her in amazement. Never in a million years would I have imagined that Mary Hanson was jealous of me.

"You've always had it all. The boyfriends, the grades, getting into college, and now you come back and everyone thinks you're the greatest. People fall in love with you wherever you go and it's NOT FAIR."

"Mary," I say gently. "That's not true."

"I saw the way Michael was looking at you. Even my own fucking fiancé is still hung up on his high school sweetheart. I'll always be second best to you," she spits

"That's not true," I say. "You were always prettier and more put together. I had to run away to have a life, you've always had everything you wanted here."

"People don't respect me the way they respect you. They don't love me the way they love you. They never will."

Before I can stop her, she drops the lighter. I watch as the flames start, low and blue in the ground and rush along the gas puddle toward the building. Within seconds, the side of the building is one fire, and the shrubs lining the back are starting to smolder.

"No! Ah!" I yell. I turn around and look for something to stop the fire. A bucket, a blanket, anything. There's nothing here. I turn back around and see Mary running back to the street. "Shit," I say under my breath. The fire is engulfing half the back of the building as the flames start to lick the windows on the second floor. I sprint to Owen's truck, jumping in the driver's seat and leaning over to pull the passenger's side door closed.

I rev the truck to life and lurch forward, away from the burning building. I need to call the fire department. I reach in my pocket and my heart drops to my stomach when I feel nothing. Swinging the truck around the corner, I glance over at the pile of papers on the passenger's seat and pat myself down to find my phone.

Nothing.

I must have left it at the hospital.

"Shit, shit, shit! Fuck!" I yell, banging my hands on the steering wheel. I turn down Main Street to the police station, driving as fast as I can. I jump out, leaving the car running and burst through the door.

"Jess!" Sheriff Wilson calls out. "To what do we owe the—"

"Fire," I pant, breathless. "The Lex is on fire."

61

OWEN

My phone starts ringing off the hook and my heart starts pounding against my ribcage. Something is wrong, I can feel it.

"Hello?"

"Owen?" Says a man's voice. I don't recognize it. He's panting, it sounds like he's running.

"Yes," I answer, frowning.

"It's Sheriff Wilson. The uh—the Lexington Hotel is on fire."

"*What?*"

"The guests have been evacuated and the fire department is on the way. Where are you?"

"I'm at the hospital."

"Are you okay?"

"I'm fine, my toe is broken," I say. I roll my eyes and sigh.

"Okay, well, we're going to send officers to you. We, uh, we suspect foul play."

My heart sinks and I take a deep breath. "What happened? Where's Jess? Is she okay?" I can hear the panic in my own voice. It sounds like Sheriff Wilson has stopped running.

"Jess is fine, she's here beside me. One second." There's some shuffling and muffled voices and finally I hear Jess's voice.

"Owen," she says.

"Jess, I was so—"

"I'm fine," she interrupts. "Have you got the laptop handy? I have your registration."

"One sec," I answer, shifting the phone to the other ear as I flip the laptop open. It seems to take forever to boot up and finally I slide the USB into the slot.

"Okay, go."

She reads out my truck registration and I click 'Done'. The password is accepted and I breathe a sigh of relief. I slide the files to attach them to the email I'd already drafted and wait as they slowly start sending. We stay on the line to each other, breathing silently while the files attach and I click send.

"Done."

"Good. Now get yourself back here. Owen," she pauses.

"What is it?"

"It was Mary. She's the one who set it on fire. I tried to stop her, but" her voice cracks. "I don't know, she just went nuts. I have the video on your dash cam, I'm not sure how much of it the camera captured. They're trying to find her now. Do you think..."

"My dad put her up to it? Absolutely." I guess that was Plan B. If he can't have a hand in my pocket, then he'd burn my pocket to the ground. My lips purse together and I shake my head. "Sheriff Wilson said he was sending some guys over to pick me up. I'll see you soon."

"How's your toe?" Jess asks after a pause.

I chuckle. "I think I'll live."

I hear her laugh softly and my heart melts. I just need to be beside her right now. I don't care about my toe, or the Lex, or my dad, or Mary, or the trial or any arrests, all I care about is her. I just want to hold her in my arms and make sure she's okay. If she's okay, if the baby's okay, then nothing else matters.

"Owen?" She says softly.

"Yeah?"

"I love you."

"I love you too Jess. Thank you," I add. "For everything."

"I'm sorry your hotel is burning down."

"I don't give a shit about the hotel. I just want you and the baby to be okay."

I hear her sob and her strangled voice says a simple "Okay."

"I'll see you soon."

"Yep," she answers in a whisper, and then the phone clicks off. I sigh and lean back in my chair. Once again, all I can do is sit back and wait and stare at those sliding glass doors.

EPILOGUE

JESS

Three weeks later...

Owen wraps his arm around my waist and kisses my temple. We watch as the last of the movers empty my grandmother's house, and I swing the small suitcase of stuff into Owen's truck. It's all I'm keeping: just a few small things from my childhood, Gram's old heirloom jewelry and her faded old apron. I'm going to get it framed and hang it up in my apartment in New York.

"That's the last of it," the mover says to me, thrusting a clipboard into my hands. "Just sign here and here and you'll get your cheque from the estate sale in a couple weeks."

I take the pen and clipboard and sign where he's pointed. I hand the clipboard back to him and he nods his head before jumping into the cab of the truck. The truck rumbles to life and Owen and I watch as they drive down the street and out of sight.

"That's everything. Sam and Ronnie signed the sale papers this morning, so that's it," I say. It feels strange to be here, in front of a house that my family no longer owns. I didn't want to keep it, so I offered it to Sam and Ronnie to buy for a fair price. She was ecstatic to be able to stay in Lexington, and I was happy to be rid of Gram's house so quickly.

"Time to move on," I say, stroking my stomach.

"Too many bad memories here," Owen says, squeezing his hand around my waist. "We get to start fresh now."

I turn to him and smile. He tilts my chin up and places a soft kiss on my lips. His lips linger against mine and I groan.

"I'll never get sick of kissing you," I say.

"Good, because neither will I." He kisses me again and I wrap my arms around his neck. "Now let's get out of this town."

A smile spreads across my face and I nod. "Okay."

We get into his truck and head off toward the highway. When we turn onto Main Street, the charred remains of the Lexington Hotel's first story rise up like an abandoned castle. Owen pulls up in front and sighs.

I laugh. "So much for the investment. Have you found any buyers for the land?"

"A developer contacted me. It's actually one of my most successful investments, between the insurance payout and the sale of the lot," he says with a raised eyebrow. "Enough to buy somewhere nice in New York. I was thinking a two or three bedroom place. You know, somewhere with room to grow?" He says the last word so tentatively and reaches his hand over toward me. He slides it over my stomach and my heart flutters.

"Are you asking me to move in with you?"

"Yeah," he nods. "Nothing would make me happier."

We stare into each other's eyes for a moment and I can feel the corners of my lips start to curl into a smile. My eyes mist up and I nod. "Okay," I say. "But let's just go to my place for a few weeks and see how we manage living together. We might hate each other."

"Doubt it," Owen says simply. He turns the truck back on and we head to the airport.

THE FLIGHT IS SMOOTH, and within a few hours we have our bags and we're at my apartment in New York City. It feels more like home than that town ever did, and with Owen by my side I feel like I couldn't be happier.

Gram's words echo in my ears and I think I know what she meant when she told me to hang onto happiness. She meant let my guard down and let this man into my life and protect what I love with all my might.

We flop onto the sofa and Owen wraps his arm around my shoulder. I turn on the TV, but before I can do anything else, he slides his other hand over my cheek and kisses me. He kisses me so passionately it feels like I've never been kissed before this. His fingers tangle into my hair and he pulls me close, but not close enough. I swing my leg on top of him so that I'm straddling him, holding onto his head and kissing him like nothing else in the world exists.

Nothing else does exist.

Owen's hands rip at my clothes, his fingers brush my skin and send sparks flying off me. His body is hot and hard underneath me and all I want is to be closer, together, more connected. Our bodies intertwine and our hearts beat side by side as our clothes evaporate into thin air. I'm in ecstasy.

My body rides wave after wave of pleasure, and Owen kisses me and tastes me and looks at me with such love in his eyes that I think we're both drunk.

Again, more than ever, I discover what it means to make

love. I discover what it means to be one with someone else and to give myself completely to them.

I discover what it means to be happy.

We savor those blissful moments after our bodies quiet down, naked and interlaced on the sofa. I rest my head against his shoulder and listen to his heartbeat as he strokes his fingers over and back along my arm.

His body stiffens slightly and he lifts his head. He looks around and finds the remote, turning the TV up until we can hear the news report.

"... McAllister has been found guilty of criminal fraud, and sentenced to fifteen years in prison. His wife will serve an eight year sentence."

I stroke his chest quietly and lift my eyes up to him.

"You okay?" I ask. He swings his gaze over to me and smiles softly.

"Yeah. It's sad, and I wish it didn't have to be this way, but they aren't the people I thought they were." He tilts my chin and kisses me deeply, before pulling away and looking deep into my eyes. "You're my family now, Jess. You and that child of ours. Even with all this," he waves at the TV, "I still feel like the luckiest man in the world."

My heart grows in my chest and I smile. In the most unlikely place, we found the family that's been missing from our lives. We found each other, and we found love.

∽

Keep reading for a preview of **Book 4: Knocked Up by the Billionaire's Son**

∽

Don't forget to grab your FREE bonus extended epilogue by signing up to my reader list:

https://www.lilianmonroe.com/subscribe

If you're already signed up, you can follow the link in your welcome email to access the bonus content from all my books.

xox Lilian

KNOCKED UP BY THE BILLIONAIRE'S SON

KNOCKED UP SERIES: BOOK 4

1

DEAN

"Sorry for the late notice, Dean, but Jeremy's called in sick. We need you for two-year-old twins' birthday party tomorrow morning at 10 a.m."

"Saturday is supposed to be my day off, Pat," I sigh. What was supposed to be a side job to give back to the community is turning into a massive time commitment.

"I know, buddy. Just help me out here. It's a cash job at a nice house, it'll pay for at least three of our non-profit events."

"Yeah, fine. No worries. Text me the address."

I hang up the phone and let out another sigh. I was looking forward to a day to myself tomorrow, but I can't back out now. It's not like I need the money, I've got loads of that. I met Pat at my niece's birthday party and found out he runs a non-profit organization for kids. I convinced him to give me a job as a children's entertainer, since working at my father's investment firm isn't exactly fulfilling. When he first offered me the job I'd laughed. 'Children's entertainer' is just a fancy way of saying 'clown'. I fell in love with the job right away, and now I love calling myself Clifford the Clown on the weekends.

I head to my closet and pull out the plastic dry-cleaner's bag hanging at the back. I unzip it and make sure everything is okay. The bright yellow suit has blue polka dots all over it with big red buttons down the front. I lay it down on my bed and pull out the suitcase with the rest of my costume and props in it. There are more than enough balloons and streamers, so all I have to do is make sure all my gear is ready to go for the morning.

It's surprisingly calming to get ready. I make sure everything is laid out for my costume and that I have enough face paint. I lay out all my balloons and games and pack them away neatly, and then I check my compressed air canister to make sure I'll be able to make balloon animals. Everything is just about in order when my phone rings again.

This better not be Pat cancelling the gig on me, I think to myself. It wouldn't be the first time it happened. As much as I love the guy and I respect what he's doing, he's not the most organized manager I've ever had. That's what you get when you work for a clown, I guess.

I pick up my phone and grimace. It's not Pat, it's worse. It's my mother.

"Mother," I say as I answer the phone.

"Dean, darling, how are you?" she asks in her honey-sweet voice.

"I'm fine, mom. What's up?"

"I just wanted to see how you were doing. I haven't spoken to you since the fundraiser last month."

Yeah, that wasn't by accident.

"I've been busy, mother. I'm doing this non-profit gig for the children's foundation."

"Of course, honey. The clown thing." I can almost hear

her waving her hand dismissively. "I just wanted to call and see if you'd spoken to Victoria lately?"

A shiver runs down my spine and I shake my head. I take a deep breath before answering and force my voice to stay even.

"Victoria and I broke up two months ago, mother. You know that."

"I know, honey, it's just that your father and I liked her so much. And the Erkharts have been so good to us over the years. It seems like a shame to throw away such a great relationship over some silliness."

Silliness? I bristle and take another deep breath to calm myself. As usual, my mother is only thinking of herself. Never mind my heartbreak or my feelings. They wouldn't matter to her. She only cares about the contacts that the Erkharts bring to their investment business.

"We broke up," I repeat. "It's over."

"Talk to her, honey," she says. I wish she'd stop calling me that. "They were over for dinner the other day and she is so *sorry* for everything that happened. She said she's just worried about you, and she's ready to forgive you for storming out on her."

"*She* is ready to forgive *me?*" I almost shout. I hear a sharp intake of breath and I try my best to stay calm. Why did my mother have my ex-fiancée over for dinner anyways? "We broke up. It's over."

"Talk to her, honey."

"Stop calling me honey," I snap.

My mother sighs. Her voice is harder when she speaks again. "You've caused us a world of pain with this breakup. Your union with Victoria was planned from the time you were two years old. We had millions tied into it. It's in your *best interest* to reconsider."

A chill goes down my spine and I resist the urge to fling my phone out the window.

"I think you're mistaking *your* best interest with *my* best interest," I spit back. *Typical of my mother, I shouldn't be surprised.* "I need to get ready for work."

"You need to get ready to put on a costume and blow up balloons, you mean," she snarls. "When are you going to grow up and realize where you come from? The only reason you're able to 'give back' is because of the sacrifices that your father and I made for you. You would have nothing without us."

"I'd have my integrity," I snap.

My mother snorts. "Right," she says. "Well, go get ready for your little job then. Call Victoria."

The phone clicks and this time I do fling it across the room. It lands on the sofa and bounces onto the floor as I put my hands against the wall and take deep breaths. I pull my arm back and smack the wall as hard as I can with my palm as a yell erupts out of me.

Why can't she understand that Victoria and I broke up? I walked in on her with another man in our own bed and she calls it 'silliness'? What universe does she live in?

With another deep breath I try to calm myself down. I go back to my bedroom and zip up the plastic bag with my costume in it and lay it across the armchair in the corner. I look at the rainbow-colored wig and the red nose in the box beside the costume and I shake my head.

What am I doing? I'm dressing up as a clown and making balloon animals on the weekends instead of putting in extra hours at the investment firm with my father. My parents tolerated the time away when I was playing by the rules, but now I can sense their patience wearing thin.

I turn back around and stomp out into the living room.

The New York skyline is glittering below me and I slump down on the sofa and put my head in my hand.

As much as I hate to admit it, my mother is right. I'm living in this penthouse because of them, and I can afford to work as a children's entertainer because of the trust fund that they set up for me. I owe them everything, but asking me to patch things up with Victoria Erkhart is just too much.

They'd never cut me off, would they? Not because I refused to marry the woman they chose for me? Surely, they love me more than that?

2

SAMANTHA

THE PLANE LANDS in New York and I glance out the window. Dusk is starting to settle and the sky is ablaze with colors. I'm like a zombie, going through the motions without really thinking about what I'm doing. Before I know it, I'm loading my bag into the back of a taxi and giving the driver Jess's address.

I glance at my big purse and see the blue manila folder sticking out of it. I turn back to the window, trying to blink back the tears that have gathered in my eyes.

Divorced.

God, I hate that word.

Or rather, soon to be divorced. As soon as I sign on the dotted line it'll be official.

The buildings rush by us and I stare through the window without seeing anything. We're on a freeway, and then we're winding through streets with tall houses all stuck together. It looks just like the movies.

It's not until the taxi driver stops the car that I blink and take a deep breath, waking up from my daze. I pay the driver and carry my suitcase up the half dozen steps to my best friend's front door. My arm is just lifting to knock on the door when it swings open.

"Sam!" she exclaims. I can't help but smile.

"Hi, Jess."

"Come in, come in. Are you hungry? Your room is down the hall on the left. Here, let me take this. How are you?"

The questions come hard and fast and I can't keep up. I just barely am able to grasp that I'm in New York, and the blue folder in my purse is burning against my side. Jess turns around as we walk down the hall and purses her lips together.

"Sorry. You must be exhausted. The twins and Owen are all asleep already. If you want to just pass out, I'll get out of your hair."

"No," I say suddenly. Jess's eyebrows raise. I try to smile. "I mean, I'd rather spend a bit of time with you. If you don't mind." *I'm not ready to be alone yet,* is what I mean to say. Jess understands right away and she smiles.

"Here's your room. Drop your suitcase and come to the kitchen. I opened a bottle of wine just in case you wanted some when you got here," she says with a wink. I try to smile again but it feels like my face has forgotten how. Jess wraps me in a hug and squeezes me close.

"It'll be okay," she whispers.

I follow her to the kitchen and we sit at the little round table in the corner. She takes out two long-stemmed wine glasses and pours generous amounts of wine in each.

"Welcome to New York," she says with a grin as she raises her glass. We clink them together and I take a sip. The rich, bitter red wine fills my mouth and I sigh in satisfaction, feeling my shoulders relax right away.

"Thank you for having me," I finally say.

Jess shakes her head. "Don't be ridiculous. When you

called, I was ready to jump on a plane myself and go down to Lexington. You shouldn't be alone right now."

I try to respond but all of a sudden there's a lump in my throat. I lift the wine up to my lips and take the tiniest sip before putting it back down. My eyelids are prickling and my heart is thumping against my ribcage.

"How did this happen?" I whisper, finally lifting my tear-filled eyes up to Jess. "How did this happen?"

Jess reaches across the table to put her hand over mine. Her eyes are soft and caring and full of concern.

"It happened when that asshole broke his vows and showed his true colors," she responds.

"What did I do wrong?" I ask, shaking my head. "I was a good wife. We weren't even married three years. I cooked and cleaned and had a job and—"

"Stop," Jess says sternly. I glance up at her, surprised. "You did nothing wrong. Do you hear me? Absolutely nothing. Cheaters cheat, that's what they do. It doesn't matter who you are or what you do, it's him who did you wrong. It's him who did it to you and it's him who is the asshole. Not you. You are a fucking saint, if you ask me," Jess says as she takes a swig of wine. "I'd have keyed his car and burned all his things in the front yard."

I feel a hint of a smile breaking my lips. Jess glances at me and grins. Her smile fades and she shakes her head. "I thought you guys were the real deal. When I went to your wedding, I thought I'd be visiting you when you were eighty with dozens of grandkids."

The tears prickle my eyes and I put my hand over my forehead. I nod, because my voice is gone. Jess reaches over and rubs my back, cooing and making soft motherly noises.

"Come on, Sam. I know it's horrible now and it feels like it will always be horrible. But it won't. Look at the bright side, you have no kids. You have skills and drive and you can get a job anywhere. The house in Lexington is paid for, so you can sell your half to Ronnie and be done with that toxic town. You have *options*," she says. I finally lift my eyes up to her and she reaches across the table to hold my hand. "So many options. You hear me?"

"I hear you, but it still feels like my life is over," I say. "That sounds so pathetic," I add with a snort.

"No, it doesn't. It sounds completely reasonable."

Jess scoots her chair over and wraps her arms around me. I lay my head on her shoulder and finally let the tears flow. I cry into her shoulder as she holds me and rocks me back and forth. Finally, when the tears start to slow down, I sit up. I take my wine and lift it to my lips to take a long drink.

"You're right," I say as I turn to Jess. A smile starts to form on her lips. "I have options."

"You do. And you can stay here as long as you want to. I mean it. As long as you want to."

I nod and smile. I don't respond because I don't trust my voice. The tears are prickling my eyes again, but this time they're tears of gratitude and love for my best friend.

"So," I clear my throat when the word comes out as a croak. "So it's the twins' birthday party tomorrow?"

Jess leans back in her chair and smiles. "Yes! Terrible twos," she laughs. "I thought the ones were terrible but apparently it gets worse!"

I laugh and shake my head. "I'm sure you'll manage."

"We will," she says with a smile, glancing down the hallway. A pang goes through my chest when I think of the partnership that Owen and Jess have. I thought I had that kind of love too—the kind of love that lasts decades. I was wrong.

"What's planned for the party?"

"We've got a clown coming!" Jess says with a laugh. "I

didn't even know they still had clowns, but apparently you can hire them by the hour. They call themselves 'children's entertainers'."

I chuckle. "That's very glamorous."

"Very," Jess adds. "Anyways, this company is supposed to be really good. I just hope the kids like it and don't end up traumatized and scared of clowns for the rest of their lives."

"Scared of children's entertainers, you mean."

Jess laughs. "Yeah, right, sorry. Children's entertainers."

I lean back in my chair and my shoulders relax again. For the first time since I left Lexington, I feel my body begin to unwind. Jess talks and we laugh until the bottle of wine is empty, and then she wraps her arms around me once again. I sigh into the hug and then we just look at each other and nod.

"See you tomorrow," she says with a smile. "Sleep tight."

"You too," I answer. I walk to my bedroom and close the door, grateful that the wine is making my eyelids heavy. I might actually be able to sleep tonight.

3

DEAN

I CRAM all my gear into the car and swear. Of course I'm late. I had three alarms set and I still slept through them. You'd think I was a fourteen year old boy and not a grown man for the amount of sleep I need. I rush back up the elevator and jump into the clown costume.

Within a few minutes, I've got the costume on and I'm painting my face. The wide red smile and bright cheeks look ridiculous, but they help me get in character. I paint the black outline and big circles around my eyes. My hair gets gelled back and my wig slides on.

I take a deep breath and look at myself in the mirror. I'm ready. I slip my regular shoes on and carry my huge clown shoes down the elevator with the last of my props. I'm finally ready. I glance at my watch and shake my head. With a bit of luck I should get there only ten or fifteen minutes late.

Traffic seems to be on my side, and I drive through the streets more quickly than anticipated. I double check the address and park in front of a house. There are balloons swinging in the wind near the front door.

"This must be it," I say to myself. I slip my big shoes on

and grab my bag of props. My hands are full but I'm able to carry everything in one trip. I slam the trunk closed and turn toward the front door.

The shoes are awkward to walk in, and I waddle my way up to the front door. I wish New York houses didn't have so many steps. I ring the doorbell and clear my throat, ready to put on my clown voice. The door swings open and a man appears on the other side.

"Clifford the clown, at your service," I say with a flourish, bowing with my arms outstretched. The man chuckles.

"Come on in, they're out back."

I follow him to the backyard and the sounds of children screaming and playing get louder. He slides the back door open and I step through. The kids turn to me immediately and start laughing. The show begins.

There's something special about performing for kids. The way their eyes shine and the way they laugh without a worry in the world makes me feel like I'm floating. Every time one of them laughs at something I do or falls for one of my pranks it feels like a mini jolt of energy to the heart.

These kids are no different. I spot the birthday twins right away: a boy and a girl. They're only two, but they're the life of the party. I give them party hats first, and then start handing them out to the other kids. I glance at the parents and hand out party hats to them as well.

As much as I didn't want to do this last night, I'm enjoying myself. I settle the kids into a semi-circle in front of me and prepare them for the balloon animal bit of my performance. I pull out the air canister and blow up a long balloon. I start twisting it and tying it as the kids watch in awe.

When Pat first started teaching me to make these, it was the most frustrating weeks of my life. It's definitely harder than it looks. It took me almost a year to get the hang of it, and I'm just now starting to feel confident.

I make the first balloon animal, a dog, and I hand it to the birthday girl.

"One for you," I say in my best Clifford the Clown voice. She giggles and waves it around and I grin. Next is a giraffe, and a monkey, and a shark. I make them one by one and hand them to the kids. By this time I'm really enjoying myself. I'm laughing along with them and I know I've got them in the palm of my hand. The adults are laughing at my jokes and I'm on a high.

I love my job.

I grab another balloon and stretch it long before starting to inflate it. Just as I start filling it with air, the sliding glass door opens and my jaw drops. She's got long brown hair that falls down well past her shoulders. Her nose has a sprinkling of freckles over it and her green eyes sparkle in the sun. She squints as she steps out, looking at me curiously. I let my eyes drop to her white tank top and tight jeans and my heart starts to race.

It's the balloon popping that brings me back to reality. It explodes in my hand and I jump. The kids jump and laugh and I pretend to fall over. They all laugh harder and I get up, pretending to struggle. I glance over at the woman. She's still standing by the door, leaning against the frame as if she's scared of getting too close to the party.

"You!" I call out to her. She stands up a bit straighter and looks over her shoulder and then back at me. "What's your favorite animal?" I ask.

She grins and shrugs.

"Come on," I say, taking a step closer. I glance back at the kids and they laugh. "You must have a favorite?"

Her smile widens and it almost knocks me over. I glance

around and see all the parents coupled off. My eyes swing to the doorway and I wonder if her husband is inside.

"Elephant," she finally says.

"Elephant," I exclaim, making a trunk with my arm for the kids and pretending to swing it around. Their laughter reaches a peak. I pull out a balloon and get to work. When I hand her the elephant, our fingers brush each other ever so gently. Even through the fabric of my white gloves I feel an electric current pass through my arm.

"Thank you," she says softly. She smiles at me and I feel my face relax. I stare at her for a few seconds before snapping back to myself. I'm Clifford the Clown right now. Dean Shelby doesn't exist. I turn back to the group of children, ready to make them laugh again. When I pull out another balloon, I can't resist turning back toward the woman. She's turning the elephant over in her hands and smiling. My heart grows in my chest.

Making a balloon elephant may be the best achievement of my life so far.

4

SAMANTHA

HE MADE the elephant so fast I could hardly tell what he was doing, but then it appeared in his hands. I run my fingers over the big ears and long trunk and shake my head. Amazing. I glance back at the clown and watch as he waves his hands over the children and they all laugh and play along.

Jess wasn't wrong, he's very good. He glances over his shoulder and our eyes meet again. He smiles at me and sticks out his tongue before turning back to the group of kids. I can feel the pulse in my whole body and I glance back down at the balloon elephant, turning it around in my hands.

"Well, look at you," Jess says with a grin. "I haven't seen you smile since you got here."

I hold up the elephant. "Guess the clown is doing his job then, huh?"

Jess's grin widens. "I guess he is."

I choose to ignore the teasing in her voice. "I didn't expect him to be so..."

"...attractive?"

"No, young!" I answer quickly. "I didn't expect him to be

so young. I thought it would be a guy in his sixties for some reason."

Jess chuckles. "So did I. It's hard to tell what he looks like under that makeup, but based on that jawline I'd say he's quite a stud."

I roll my eyes. "Aren't you married?"

Jess grins at me. "I'm not looking for me, Sam," she says.

"Stop," I say. "I'm not even divorced yet. I'm not ready."

"Whatever you say," she replies. I glance back at the clown and try to imagine what his face would look like. He lifts his arms and the fabric of his costume pulls across his broad back. He's certainly muscular.

"Harper, Rosie!" Jess calls over. "Come over here and help me settle something."

"What are you doing," I whisper. She looks at me and grins again. The two women come closer and Jess nods to the clown.

"What do you think about Clifford? You think he's a hunk under all that makeup?"

Rosie and Harper turn toward the clown and suddenly all four of us are staring at him. Rosie tilts her head to the side and Harper squints.

"Definitely," Rosie says. "Certified stud." She turns back toward us and nods once, as if that's the official seal of approval. Jess laughs.

"I knew it. See, Sam? You should go for it!"

"Absolutely," Harper says. "The best way to get over someone is to get under someone else. I've never had sex with a clown before."

I start laughing and shake my head. "Stop, stop! I'm not sleeping with anyone!" I know they're only joking but I can't help the blush that starts to creep over my cheeks. Jess puts an arm around my shoulder and laughs.

"I'm only teasing. No harm in looking though. Come on, let's get you a drink."

She pulls me toward the kitchen and I steal one last glance toward Clifford the Clown. He's got the kids all lined up and somehow is getting them to jump and move exactly as he says. He definitely has a gift for working with children.

The four of us step inside and I listen as Harper, Rosie, and Jess talk about their kids. They laugh and joke about all the things that kids do, and I can't help but feel like the odd one out. Not only do I not have a child, but my marriage has been an absolute disaster.

The lightness that I felt when I was watching the clown perform starts to dissipate as thoughts about Ronnie creep in. I still remember the way he looked when I confronted him. He denied everything even though I had followed him to the restaurant and seen him kiss her. My whole world had crumbled around me.

He must have been cheating on me for months, maybe even longer. My throat tightens and I try to push the thoughts away when Jess appears beside me with a glass of chilled white wine.

"Here," she says with a whisper. "If I have one job today, it'll be to get you to drink and smile." She looks up and toward the back door. "Where's Clifford? He was good at that."

I laugh and shake my head as Jess nudges my shoulder. The two other girls laugh. Just then, the laughter and children's screams outside get a little bit higher pitched. I hear an adult yell. The four of us look at each other and then rush outside.

It's carnage. I don't know how this happened in such a short amount of time. Clifford the clown is on the ground, holding his arm and writhing around. The kids are running around in circles and Owen is trying to wrangle them. Matt, Jess's son, is swinging a plastic baseball bat wildly over and back. He knocks the clown's air canister and it falls with a loud clang.

Owen finally manages to grab Matt just as Jess starts herding the other children together. I jog over to the clown as he lies on the ground.

"You okay?" I say as he groans. His eyes slowly lift up to me and he blinks a few times.

"Yeah, yeah, I'm fine," he says and then groans as he tries to stand up. "My arm."

"What's wrong? What happened? We were only gone for a minute."

"That's all it takes," he says with a grimace. His regular voice is deep and gravelly. Despite all the clown makeup, something sparks between my legs. Even with all the clown makeup, I can see the way his eyes gleam when he smiles. "That one grabbed a bat and hit me," he says, nodding toward Matt. "I tripped over these stupid shoes and fell on my arm. I think it might be broken."

"Oh my goodness," I say softly. "Come on."

I help him to his feet and guide him to the kitchen. Soon, he's got some ice on his arm and he's sighing. I grab a dish towel and wrap it around his arm in a makeshift sling.

"There," I say.

"Are you a nurse?" He asks as he admires my handiwork. I laugh.

"No, not a nurse. Just resourceful." I study his face for a minute before speaking again. "I'm Sam," I say after a pause.

"Clifford," he replies as his eyes spark again.

"Wait, is that your real name?" I ask as I try to hide the smile on my lips. He lets out a quick laugh and shakes his head.

"Dean Shelby," he says as he extends his good hand. "Nice to meet you."

The instant our hands touch it's like a current of electricity passes through my arm. His eyes are locked on mine and it feels like time stops.

He clears his throat. "Thank you," he says, motioning to the sling. He shifts his weight and groans. "This is so painful."

"You're going to have to go to the hospital," Jess says as she comes back in through the door. I almost jump backward. "I'm so sorry about this."

"It's fine," he says. He glances at me and winks. "Occupational hazards."

I can't help but laugh. "Dangerous job," I say.

"Very."

Jess glances at his arm and shakes her head. She puts her hands on her hips and sighs. "I'm so sorry, Clifford. So, so sorry. Can you drive? I'll call you a cab. I'm so sorry."

"I have a stick shift," he answers with a grimace. "So, no, I guess."

"I'll drive," I hear myself say. "I can drive stick and none of these kids are mine. I don't mind."

"Are you sure?" the clown says, knitting his eyebrows together. It gives his face an exaggerated sad look and I start laughing.

"She's sure," Jess responds with a raised eyebrow. "Here," she says, handing me some money. "For the cab back."

"Don't worry about it, Jess." I say with a smile.

"Then you take it," she says, thrusting the money into Clifford's sling. "For this whole mess. Call it a tip."

He just laughs and shakes his head. "It's really not necessary. It's fine, really. Kids get excited and it happens."

"Just take it," she says. "I feel so bad. I'm so sorry."

"Don't be." He grimaces again and I stand up a bit straighter.

"Come on," I say. "We should get you to the hospital sooner rather than later." I hook my arm around his shoulder and try to ignore the thrill that passes through me when our bodies touch. He groans as he stands up and then looks at the sling and nods approvingly.

"Let's go," he says, letting his eyes linger on mine for just a few moments. I blush and look away, not daring to look at him or Jess.

∾

You can get the full version of Knocked Up by the Billionaire's son by copying this link into your browser:
https://www.amazon.com/dp/B07M6LCQ7G

Don't forget, you can get exclusive access to bonus chapters for ALL my books.
https://www.lilianmonroe.com/subscribe

∾

ALSO BY LILIAN MONROE

For all books, visit:

www.lilianmonroe.com

Brother's Best Friend Romance

Shouldn't Want You

Military Romance

His Vow

His Oath

His Word

The Complete Protector Series

Enemies to Lovers Romance

Hate at First Sight

Loathe at First Sight

Despise at First Sight

Secret Baby Romance:

Knocked Up by the CEO

Knocked Up by the Single Dad

Knocked Up... Again!

Knocked Up By the Billionaire's Son

The Complete Knocked Up Series

Knocked Up by Prince Charming

Knocked Up by Prince Dashing

Knocked Up by Prince Gallant

Knocked Up by the Broken Prince

Knocked Up by the Wicked Prince

Knocked Up by the Wrong Prince

Fake Engagement/ Fake Marriage Romance:

Engaged to Mr. Right

Engaged to Mr. Wrong

Engaged to Mr. Perfect

Mr Right: The Complete Fake Engagement Series

Mountain Man Romance:

Lie to Me

Swear to Me

Run to Me

The Complete Clarke Brothers Series

Extra-Steamy Rock Star Romance:

Garrett

Maddox

Carter

The Complete Rock Hard Series

Sexy Doctors:

Doctor O

Doctor D

Doctor L

The Complete Doctor's Orders Series

Time Travel Romance:

The Cause

A little something different:

Second Chance: A Rockstar Romance in North Korea

∼

Printed in Great Britain
by Amazon